Table of C

© Copyright 2020 by Lilly Wilder All rights reserved.

In no way is it legal to reproduce, duplicate, or transmit any part of this document in either electronic means or in printed format. Recording of this publication is strictly prohibited and any storage of this document is not allowed unless with written permission from the publisher. All rights reserved.

Respective authors own all copyrights not held by the publisher.

Wolf's Mate

By: Lilly Wilder

Foreword

I've always been a good girl, a sheltered girl. I guess I have my extremely rich dad to thank for that. Outside of his home, I want to escape the reputation that follows our name, but you can never get the stink of money off of you, no matter how hard you try. It's a smell that attracts hungry beasts... just like blood.

The one time I finally decide to let go and live a little, something bad happens. Something horrible. I find unlikely protectors in the two wolf shifters who save me, but they want something in return. Their clan is in danger of dying out, unless they find mates willing to produce offspring.

Desperate and afraid, I need to stay hidden, so they offer to protect me, but at what cost? They want a good girl to break the rules. But, can she?

Wolf's Mate

CHAPTER 1

I've just finished putting some red nail polish on my toes, when I hear a knock on the door. I don't even lift my head. I can guess who it is by the sound of the voice. Also, this house is huge enough to accommodate five families, but unfortunately, only one, or perhaps, half of one, lives here.

"Come in!" I shout, blowing softly at my reddened nails.

I know no one will be seeing them, but that's not my concern right now. I'm mostly doing them so I can take focus from other, much more important things that are happening to me right now, and the red nails are among the few things I can control.

"Are you decent, sweetheart?"

I see my father covering his eyes with the palm of his hand, as he steps in the doorway. I chuckle to myself. He's like a vampire, who can only come in if you invite him. Otherwise, his feast of blood might not be open for the night.

"Yes, I'm decent, dad. Come in," I repeat.

He uncovers his eyes and walks in. When he talks like this, he makes me feel like I'm still in high school. But, I guess daughters always remain little girls in the eyes of their parents. Especially their fathers.

I glance up only a little, as he keeps walking over to the bed, a little ceremoniously. As always, his hand brushes the photo frame on the nightstand to my bed, the one that is encasing the loving face of my late mother, his late wife. It's been ten years already, and it's not true what they say. Time doesn't make it better. The wound is still as fresh as it was ten years ago, when we got a call from the hospital that she was in a car accident. It was a hit and run. Whoever did it, didn't even stop to check up on her. They just drove away, leaving her there alone, in pain, on the road.

I shudder at the thought, like I always do. I wonder if she called out to me, to dad. What were her last words, her last thoughts? And, most importantly, how come no one helped her? It still hurts, and I'll never get used to the lack of her presence, but eventually, you realize you need to move on, even if everything reminds you of that pain. You just have to keep going, despite everything. If pain is all you see, you just become that pain. You incorporate it into your existence, into your very essence. That is how you continue.

My dad sits on the bed next to me. He's already dressed to the nines. I see he's wearing the Dormeuil Vanquish II suit, which he recently got on some auction. He's been spending more money on frivolous things lately, but what are you supposed to do when you're a widower, but you're still not old enough to kick the bucket? I remember he mentioned that this particular suit cost him $95,319, and the reason why it's so expensive is simple. It's made of five of the world's most pricey and rarest fabrics: royal Qivuik, Ambassador, Dorsilk, Kirgzy White, and Fifteen Point Eight. The mayor is throwing a gala tonight, and anyone who is anyone is invited. No wonder he wants to wear it for the occasion.

"That looks very nice on you, dad."

"You think so?" he wonders, straightening out his shoulders a little.

I see it's been immaculately pressed, and smells of lily in the valley. Gina probably had the honors of taking it to that special dry cleaning place, over in Woodlington. Dad only trusts those guys with his expensive suits. So did mom.

"Are you sure I can't convince you to change your mind and come with me?" he asks, seeing I'm not replying.

"Seriously, dad. Like, more than 90% of people there will be old. And, by old I mean older than you."

"Thanks for that," we both chuckle. "Yeah, I guess it's just one of those fundraisers that are fun only for those who actually get the money in the end."

"I thought you were giving money this time."

"Eh, with me it's always a little bit of both," he winks at me.

His hair has gotten grey, and the lines on his face are deeply set. And, it's gotten worse in the last five years. Still, he's wearing his contacts now, instead of glasses. Mom tried to convince him to switch for ages, and he only listened to her when she was gone.

"Will it be a quiet night at home for you?" he asks.

Sometimes, I mind it. Because, I'm not a little girl anymore. No matter what he thinks. But, at the same time, I understand. I'm all he's got left. Just me, and a shitload of money that is piling up in some Swiss bank account, that no one will really get to spend apart from me and him. And, it looks like neither of us is all that eager for that luxury.

"You're all packed, I see."

He looks around and notices the suitcases in the corner. I sigh. I know he wants me to stay here. He feels like this is the only place where I will be 100% safe. Or maybe, that's only because he'll be able to keep an eye on me almost all the time. Fathers and daughters, I guess. He always wants to be my protector.

But, I keep telling him that this is how life goes. Kids move out. This is good. I need my own space. I'm starting a new job as a personal assistant to Mrs. Lindbergh, the lady who owns Modern Fashion magazine. He knows that job is a dream come true, and it was hard for him not to interfere. All he needed to do was make one phone call and the job would be mine. That's the good thing about being the daughter of a multi-millionaire.

But, that's also the bad thing. You never know if you got something because you deserved it, or just because someone wants something from you. It's a world of favors. A world of I scratch your back and you scratch mine. A world where you need to be wary of what others tell you to your face, because they might be saying the exact opposite behind your back.

I guess my mother taught me differently. She never came from money, and she had to work hard for what she had. Even when she and dad hit it big, she never forgot where she came from. That takes a lot of character, and she had it. She told me to always do my best and rely on my own resources. Money will only get you so far. But, your own skills can take you all the way, wherever you want to end up.

So, I made him promise not to interfere, and as far as I know, he didn't. I still got the job, but now, I can be proud about it.

"Yup, all packed," I smile. His smile is a little sour. "Don't be sad." I pinch his cheek. "Not like I'll be moving away to another continent."

"I don't think I'd be able to handle that," he tells me, and I know he means it.

"That's why I'm moving only a few streets down, silly. I need to spread my wings and fly out of the nest. It's high time, don't you think?"

I wrap my arms around him, not waiting for him to reply. He hugs me back, and we remain like that for a moment. His eyes are deep, pensive. I wonder what he's thinking about. Is it the gala or something else?

"I'll wrinkle your suit," I pull back, making sure he still looks presentable.

"You're the only one who's allowed to do that, kiddo."

"Have fun, tonight," I wave as he heads to the door, then suddenly stops.

"How about we have breakfast at that little French bakery, before you start unloading tomorrow?" he suggests.

I will order a latte with a chocolate croissant. He will have bagels and black coffee. Mom always had something different. She liked to try out anything new that they baked. She was just like that.

"You mean the boulangerie?" I tried pronouncing it as mom would, and we both smiled at my unsuccessful attempt at it.

"Yes, that's the one," he nods.

"I'd like that," I speak, and I feel my eyes water a little.

Seeing him like that, I want to tell him that I'm not moving, that I'd stay with him and nothing would change. I regress back into my childhood, back in the good old days when his arms were the safest place on earth, and no matter what happened, my mother's voice would soothe me. In those days, everything would turn out alright eventually. Unfortunately, the present day wasn't like that. It was occasionally fun, occasionally gloomy. But, you had to go on.

Despite that inner feeling, I stay where I am, for the time being. He nods, as if he expected me to say something else, then silently walks out of the door. The house is vast and empty, as usual.

I look at my bare feet. The nail polish is scraped in more than one place. But, I'm too lazy to fix that. I lie down on the bed, letting the softness of the mattress envelop me, like a pair of loving arms. I think about my new job, and how exciting it will be. My hopes are soaring.

I close my eyes, and drift off to sleep. I dream, but I rarely remember. Maybe, it's for the better.

I don't know this yet, but this will be the last time I'll sleep in this bed. This will be the last time I feel safe...for a long time.

CHAPTER 2

The following day goes by quickly, and in a blink of an eye, it's evening. All of my stuff has been moved to my new place, courtesy of the moving company dad hired for me, even though I said a few times that I could arrange it myself. When I close the door to the last moving guy, I take a deep breath as I look around.

I love this place. I absolutely love it. Technically, it's not really mine because I'm just renting it, but it still feels like mine. The little touches here and there helped me adopt it as my very own. My mom always said that a house is just four walls that keep you safe from the weather. But, a home is a place of warmth, where you are reminded at every step that you live here, that you are safe here. I placed a framed photo of all three of us right by my bedside, and I scattered little trinkets, dust collectors as dad likes to refer to them, all throughout the apartment. Sure, it'll be a bother to clean up, having to move them all then put them back in the same place. But, it feels like home. It truly does.

An idea comes to mind. I could invite dad over and we could order some pizza. But, before I can even reach for my phone, I hear the doorbell. I look in the direction of the door and smile. Could he have predicted my idea and is now standing in front of the door?

I walk over there and unlock it, but upon opening, I see, with a slight dash of disappointment, that it's not him.

"Hey, girl!" Tina shouts at me so loudly that the whole hallway echoes. I've grown accustomed to her in your face manners and stopped being bugged, even though I know others find it somewhat crude.

Tina, unlike Nicoletta who is standing right next to her, isn't from our social circles. At least, she didn't start out that way. She was just a country bumpkin, a term Nicky and I use endearingly, and Tina doesn't like it, but she puts up with it, but then her dad hit it big on the stock market and moved the whole family to the big city. All three of us found ourselves in the same class in high school, and we somehow clicked.

"Hey, guys," I reply, moving to the side to let them in.

Nicky walks in first, and I see she's ready for a night out in a sequeny top and a mini skirt, slightly too short for my taste. Nicky's always had a body to show, and she had no problem flaunting it. Even back when she was still jail bait, she'd walk in those high heels she stole from her mother's closet like a pro, with a thin cigarette hanging low from the corner of her full lips.

"You all done unpacking?" Nicky asks, glancing around.

Tina sits on the sofa. The way she's dressed, you'd think she's about 5 years younger than Nicky, in those plain jeans and white blouse. I see she's not wearing her glasses, either. That usually means she's going out and wants to meet someone new.

"Sort of," I nod. "What are you guys doing here? I thought we arranged to meet up tomorrow."

"That plan is still on," Nicky nods. "But Tina and I were thinking that you moving out of that mansion deserves a celebration. I mean, I still don't know what possessed you to do this, that house is freakin' amazing, but all the more power to you."

Tina chuckles on the sofa and from this angle, I see the skin on her chin thickening. In about 10, 20 years, she'll be overweight like her mother, if she's not careful.

"So, we're taking you to the Winchester," Nicky concludes.

Winchester is exactly what its name says. Owning up to the name of a gun that won the West, Winchester is a club that quickly became the most popular hangout of the young and affluent. Also, it was no slave to stereotypes. You had the money to pay for the insanely expensive drinks you order? Then, come on in.

"Oh, guys, I'm not really in the mood for elbowing my way through the crowd to get to the bathroom, or guys shouting lame pickup lines in my ear," I roll my eyes, sitting down next to Tina.

"Remember the s'more guy?" Tina giggles.

"Are you a campfire? Cuz you're hot and I want s'more!" Nicky alters her voice as she's speaking, deepening it a little as she speaks, and we are all bursting with laughter. None of us remembers what the poor guy looked like; we just remember his pickup line. And, with a lame one like that, it's better we don't remember anything more.

"How can you not want to hear more gems like that?" Nicky smirks.

I turn to Tina, and I see her giving me the puppy dog eye look. Nicky has slid right next to me on the sofa, and they're pressing onto me from both sides.

"Pleeeeeeeasse?" they chant in unison, and I finally jump up.

"Alright, alright!" I laugh. "But, just one drink."

"Hallelujer! Praise the Lort! " Nicky does her best Madea voice, and we're all rolling.

"Just give me a minute to change," I say, when I finally stop laughing.

"Put on that slutty black dress!" I hear Nicky shout. "I want some competition this time!"

I always think that Tina might take it the wrong way and get upset or something, because Nicky really doesn't have a filter. Once, she even told me that my dad was hot for an old guy and if she was drunk enough, she'd bang him. Needless to say, sleepovers were off from that day on. Not that I'd think she'd really do it. Sometimes, Nicky was just a show off. All bark and no bite. But, with things like that you can never be 100% sure.

About an hour later, we're elbowing our way through the Winchester. It's always busy, but tonight is ridiculously so. I regret agreeing to this, but I couldn't say no to my best friends who came to celebrate this special moment in my life with me. So, I figured, one drink couldn't hurt.

I lean onto the bar, and realize that Nicky already caught hold of some guy and they're dirty dancing, hands sliding everywhere. Alright then, Nicky's out. Tina is still by my side, but I know she'll be gone the moment she starts batting her long eyelashes and someone walks over, which won't take long. I order us both drinks, and one for Nicky if she decides to join us at some later point. By the time I take my first sip, I feel Tina's hand squeezing my shoulder and pointing at a guy across the bar from us, raising his glass to her. And, that means I'm on my own. I thought it'd take a bit longer this time, but never mind. I'll just finish my drink in peace, hopefully devoid of lame pickup lines, I'll dance a little, then call an Uber home and be in bed at a still reasonable time.

"Looks like your posse left you hanging," I hear someone shout right into my ear, trying to be louder than the music blasting all around us.

"Excuse me!?" I turn around, giving whoever said that a dirty look. He didn't just say what I think he did, did he?

"I said," the slick-haired, smile-adorned guy leans a little closer to me, and his cologne floods down my nostrils and my throat, as he speaks, "looks like your posse left you hanging!"

"Oh," I nod, instinctively moving a little back. "Yeah. They're just having fun."

I'm about to turn my back to him again, a subtle effort at nipping whatever this is in the bud, but he won't have it.

"Are you?" I hear him ask.

"Am I what?"

"Having fun?"

My body turns fully to him now. I even slide my drink to my right side, so I can reach it easily, without turning away from him. He's not that bad looking. Slightly rugged, rocking that 3 day old beard like he just forgot to shave and doesn't care. I'm guessing he's a little hot in that black leather jacket, but guys, just like girls, are willing to sacrifice comfort for looking good. Underneath the jacket, I see the faint outlines of a Nirvana t-shirt. So, we got a rebel on our hands.

"I'm alright," I reply. "You?" I ask, not really because I'm desperate to prolong this conversation, but out of sheer politeness. He hasn't started off with a lame pick up line, and that counts for something, too.

"I am, but I don't like seeing a beautiful woman alone at a bar. Just seems wrong to me."

"Does it now?" I chuckle.

The music has gotten more bearable, and we can have an actual conversation without invading too much of our personal space.

"What are you drinking?"

"A Manhattan," I tell him.

He immediately signals at the bartender to bring me another one.

"You didn't have to do that," I tell him, now looking at two glasses of drinks I might not finish.

"I only have to do one thing, and that is die," he grins, "eventually. Everything else I do is led by pure desire."

"At least you're honest about it," I can't help but join in this little flirting.

"Why lie?" he shrugs. "We're all animals. Only, some are better at hiding it than others."

"Homo homini lupus est?" I smirk, remembering the little Latin I had back in high school, and the only proverb that stuck for some reason.

He frowns a little, tilting his head to the left side. He takes a long, drawn out inhale through his nostrils, which expand abnormally for just one single moment. Then, his lips purse, as his nostrils take their normal form again. It all happened so quickly, that I'm left wondering if I just imagined seeing that.

"Not many girls can quote Latin," he says, those grey eyes taking over a depth that hasn't been there before. "And, good Latin. What other surprises have you got hiding in that pretty little head of yours?" He gets so close to me, that the very fragrance of his cologne makes me woozy. Immediately, I remember all those horror stories about guys drugging the girls they meet at bars by putting something in their drinks, but I'm sure that he hasn't touched mine. Still, why am I feeling like I'm drunk after half a Manhattan?

"I don't reveal that after just one drink," I hear myself chuckle, but it's like it's not me, like I'm hearing myself from some deep cave and my voice is all distorted.

"More drinks could be arranged," his grin has turned into a sneer.

His eyes are leering, and his fangs seem to have grown longer. But, it can't be. People can't grow their teeth. I just haven't noticed them before, because I haven't been looking at him closely enough.

"Thank you, but I plan on finishing the one I ordered for myself, and heading on home," I manage to mutter, fighting off a wave of tiredness.

I feel like I could lie down on the ground, close my eyes and just fall asleep. I've never felt this before, and it's alarming. Something's not right. I look around, looking for either Tina or Nicky, but they're nowhere to be seen.

"Looking for someone?" he asks.

"Yeah, my posse, as you called them."

"Want me to help you look for them?"

His offer catches me off guard. I don't know why he's so insisting. Usually, guys can sense when you're not interested and most of them leave you alone. This one, however, isn't giving up, so more serious measures are obviously needed.

"Listen - "

"Sven."

"Sven?" I repeat, with a smile that threatens to give him more hope.

"Nordic parents," he shrugs, and that leather jacket follows suit.

"Of course, Sven," I continue, "you seem like a nice guy and everything, but I've had a super busy week, and I just want to find my friends, so I can say goodbye and head on home."

I've lost all desire for that drink that still stared at me from the bar. I just want to cuddle in my new bed and read my book before bedtime.

"You put it very nicely," he replies with a smile that shows no threat, but those fangs still seem longer than before, and that dizziness inside my head isn't letting go. "So, I won't bother you. Just wanted to help you out, in case you needed it. But, you obviously don't."

I don't say anything to that, but I'm glad this won't end in drama. Hopefully, I'll be home, locking the doors to my new place in less than half an hour.

"Can I just... no, sorry... it's stupid."

"What is it?" I ask, feeling a little guilty. He did back down immediately when I asked him to.

"I just wanted to give you a hug."

I think about it for a moment or two, but I already see him leaning in with open arms, so I give in. The hug lasts a little longer than I would have liked it to, but once he lets go, I smile, wave awkwardly, and disappear in the crowd, thanking my lucky stars I got out of that one so easily.

I find Nicky all over her new guy, and I have to poke her on the shoulder. She turns and is surprised to see me. I lean in to tell her I'm heading home.

"Home?" she shouts. "No! Stay!"

I shake my head, patting my watch, pretending it's already too late. I give her a peck on the cheek.

"You'll be fine?" she shouts again, and I just nod once more.

I do the same with Tina, only she's even more reluctant to let me go home alone, but I see that she also found some entertainment for tonight, and I don't want to ruin anyone's good time. I hug her as well, and head on out.

Once feeling the fresh air around me again, I inhale deeply. I slide my purse from my right shoulder, and open it easily. Nicky has mentioned it a few times that the clasp is too loose and it can be opened way too easily, even by someone who isn't trying all that hard. But, it's a bag that belonged to my mother, so I'm not changing it. Not like I don't have several expensive ones gathering dust in my closet. But, they're nowhere near as valuable as this one.

I fumble inside, trying to find my phone. After a few scoops with my hand, I still end up with nothing apart from my wallet and keys. My bags and purses are never full of shit, like it's the case with Nicky's bags, where you can even find living breathing things in there. Mine are usually light and with just a few basic necessities. On this particular night, I made sure not to take anything, apart from those 3. Now, I realize I have only two.

Confused, I take out my wallet and check the insides. Everything's there. Some cash, my cards, a few notes. Nothing is missing. I hear my keys jangle inside, so I take those out, too. I look inside, and see only emptiness. My phone is gone. I put the keys and the wallet inside, and rake my fingers through my hair, breathing in deeply.

Did I leave it anywhere? Did I even take it with me? I have a vague recollection of putting it inside with the other things, but that's as reliable as being sure I locked the front door every time I went out. It's an instinctual action, one I rarely do focused, so it's difficult to remember if I really did it this time. But, one is sure. My phone isn't on me. I'll go home and check if it's there. If it's not, I'll just remotely switch it off and try to find it. However, I still have to get home, and with a dozen people outside, waiting for a cab, it'll be tricky getting one.

With the corner of my eye, I see someone's cigarette light up in the opposite alleyway, so I look up. I see Sven, who isn't looking my way, or at least seems like he isn't. A moment later, and our eyes meet. He smiles, hesitates, and then walks over to me.

"I'm really not stalking you," he tells me.

I'm not sure if I believe that. "Oh really?" I smile.

"Just went out for a smoke. My friends are back in, found some girls. You know how it goes."

"Mhm," I nod.

"Everything OK? You look... I don't know. A little freaked out. Is it me?" he takes a step back. "If it is, I'll just leave you alone. I know how this looks. First we talked, you blew me off, and now I'm here, outside, at the same time you are."

"No, no," I shake my head. "It's not you. I think I lost my phone."

"Here?"

"It's either that or I left it at home."

"Let's hope it's that."

"Yeah," I sigh. "But, at this rate, I'll never catch a cab, and can't call an Uber."

"You want a ride?"

The moment he asks that, I realize he's regretted it. I appreciate it, but I'm not in the habit of going with guys I just met and letting them drive me wherever. My parents taught me better than that.

"Sorry, just trying to be nice."

"I know," I manage a smile. "And, I appreciate it. I really do. But, maybe you could just lend me your phone so I can call a cab or an Uber?"

"Absolutely." He quickly reaches into his pocket and extracts a small, thin silver phone. "Here you go."

"Thanks."

I call an Uber, and it tells me it should arrive in less than 10 minutes. The guy who answered didn't mind when I explained the situation, saying I'm not using my own account and will be paying cash, instead of being charged to my account. I hang up the phone and give it back to Sven.

"You know, we've been talking all this time, and I still don't know your name," he suddenly tells me, throwing away the butt of his cigarette and stepping on it with the tip of his shoes.

"It's Maddie," I offer him my hand. I guess, it doesn't matter anymore. We'll be strangers again in ten minutes or less.

"Nice to meet you, Maddie," he shakes it. "You know, I almost feel bad I have to do this."

"Do what?"

I immediately let go of his hand. The flicker in his eyes has become ominous, threatening. I haven't been threatened many times in my life, but I know the feeling. It's instinctual. You can recognize a sense of danger even if you've never been in one.

I see him looking over my shoulder, and I realize that the sounds around us have died down. There aren't many people around, if any. It's a dark alley, with no traffic, no people. I could be swallowed by the dark and no one would be any wiser.

I feel my throat getting parched, and I take a step back.

"I wouldn't do that if I were you," he shakes his index finger at me. "My friends are with your girlfriends, and all it takes is one sign from me, and they'll hurt them."

His words ring in my ear, like an echo of a horrible song.

"What do you want from me?" I muster.

"I want you to take a ride with me," he says calmly.

His hands are empty. He has no weapon, no gun, and no knife. I could just run away, run back in or down the street. But, I don't do any of those things. I'm frozen in place, unable to move. It's like he's keeping me in place with his stare alone.

"Where are you taking me?"

"If I tell you that, I'll have to kill you," he grins, and I notice his fangs are shiny and pointy, like a wolf's. His square jaw protrudes, as his smirk becomes more hostile. "And, I really don't want to hurt you, unless I have to."

He takes a step closer to me. I want to move back, but I can't. He's so close to me now, his teeth bared right in the soft area of my neck. Images of Count Dracula are evoked in my mind, and I expect him to dig into me any second. But, he doesn't. My fingers tremble as he takes my hand into his, interlocking our fingers.

"See? Your own body doesn't want to listen to you. It's listening to me," he whispers. "It knows that you won't run away, because you don't want to."

My heart is beating like crazy, and I have no idea why I'm still here, why I'm not back inside, screaming for help. My legs aren't my own anymore. My mind has been invaded by this monster from the dark. Against all common sense, I take a step closer to him, and it feels like the most natural thing to do. My nostrils are filled with a musky, masculine scent, and I feel it infiltrating every inch of the insides of my body, while he just keeps grinning at me, whispering in some silent, unknown language that doesn't seem to spill out of his lips, but emanates from somewhere inside of me.

"My car is over there," I hear him say.

I don't follow. I float, like a balloon, my steps as light as air, as this stranger takes me to his car, and my body can't do anything but comply.

CHAPTER 3

I must have dozed off, and my head bumping against the car window wakes me up. I look outside, and recognize no landmarks of the city, which I grew up in. All I see are vast fields of nothing, that seem to merge with the endless sky somewhere in the distance, and even if there was a chance of me running away, I wonder where I would run.

I swallow heavily, as I lean back into the car seat. I can breathe more clearly now, my nose feels freed from that oppressive smell that lingered back in the alleyway. Instinctively, I try the door, but of course, it's locked. I hear a chuckle from the driver's seat.

"You don't think it would be that easy, do you, princess?"

I don't need to look up at the rearview mirror to recognize that voice. It is the voice that will never leave my mind, no matter how hard I try, the voice that will continue to ring on through my nightmares probably for as long as I'm alive.

His eyes glisten in the darkness, the grey hue becoming even lighter now. He occasionally looks up to check on me, but doesn't say much else. I rest my trembling hand on my thighs, trying to calm my breathing. When we stop somewhere and he opens the car door, I could push him away and just run. Run anywhere, it doesn't matter. Anywhere is safer than with this lunatic, whoever he is. I don't want to stick around to find out why he has me in a car or where he's taking me.

But, I eventually do. Our ride is short, and he stops in front of some old, military-looking, abandoned facility. There is not a single soul alive here. The silence echoes in the trees, and I know that, even if I shouted at the top of my voice, no one will hear me, no one will come to my rescue.

Still sitting in the driver's seat, he turns to me and throws a pair of metallic handcuffs into my lap, which are as cold as his glare.

"Put them on," he instructs, as if I've done this a million times before and I know exactly how one puts on handcuffs.

Slowly, my fingers barely able to unclasp and open them up, I secure one side to my left wrist first, then with some slight maneuvering, I attach my other wrist, with an equal sound of lost freedom. I lift my hands up in the air for him to see.

"Good girl," he smirks. "I'll make sure to tell your father you've been most cooperative."

"My father?" I whisper, but he's already out of the car and walking over to my side to open the door.

He helps me out surprisingly gently, then gestures at me to walk towards the dilapidated building in front of us.

"Where are we going?" I ask, even though I realize how futile that question is.

"You just keep being a good girl, and no harm will come to you," he explains, answering my second, unspoken question. "That also depends on how your father reacts to my deal."

"What deal?" I cry as he pushes me inside the dark engulfed building, and I expect monster hands from all sides reaching at me, threatening to tear me apart. But, no hands attack me and instead, Sven just turns on the light.

The place is empty, apart from a few cardboard boxes in the corner, and a table with a single chair right in the middle of the big, cement-floored room.

"Take a seat there," he urges me.

He watches me fulfil his command with a steady gaze. His hand reaches into his pocket, and extracts a box of half empty cigarettes. He takes out one and lights it up. Once he's seen me sit down, he walks over to the other end of the table. His hand once again dives into his left pocket, and this time, what surfaces isn't cigarettes. It's my phone.

Eyes wide open, I stare at my phone, then him, then back at my phone again.

"I had to make sure that you didn't call for help," he explains, as if we're discussing the weather and he's wondering whether he should bring an umbrella tomorrow, because it might rain.

My blood runs cold listening to him. How many times has he done something like this? He probably wants to call my father to ask for ransom money. Despite what my father thinks, I remember what happened when I was 4 years old. They're just snippets in my mind, and sometimes, it feels like it happened to someone else. I guess, that's how the brain copes with the fact that I was moments away from being taken away from my parents and everything I knew. I was playing on the swings, while my mother was watching me. As they say, all it takes is a single moment of no one paying attention, and tragedy can happen. The man had a long coat, which smelled like tobacco, like it was growing in his inside pockets. His hands were stained yellow. They were rough, coarse. When he grabbed me by the wrist, he almost scratched me. The car he was pulling me towards was bright red, like those balloons little kids get at fairs. I remember not even realizing what was happening. Then, my mother screamed. Then, commotion. The coarse hand let go of me, and I lost sight of the bright red car, once I was back in my mother's safe arms.

We never spoke of that, none of us. I guess my parents believed I was too young to remember, and there was no point in stirring old memories that might trigger trauma. It's better to keep them buried. Even now, after all these years, when these images come flooding back, I can almost fully convince myself that it happened to someone else. But, that tiny voice in the back of my mind knows. And, it doesn't even shut up.

"Now, we are going to call your father," Sven tells me, finishing his cigarette and stomping it with his foot, a little agitated.

He makes me unlock my phone with my fingerprint, and he finds my dad's number easily. He puts it on speaker phone, and lays it on the table before me. It rings only twice before my dad picks up.

"Sweetheart, is everything alright?" I hear concern in his voice.

But, before I can reply, Sven does it for me. "I'm afraid sweetheart is a bit tied up at the moment," he explains, leaning a little towards the table.

"Who is this?" my father's tone changes from concerned, to frantic, to pissed off.

"I'm surprised, shocked even, to see you don't recognize the voice of your old time friend, Hugo."

A moment of silence follows, and I can picture that look on my father's face, like someone showing him a veiled box, then suddenly pulling the veil off, revealing the contents.

"Sven?" my father's voice is not nearly as big as it was a second ago. "Is that you?"

"Who else could it be?" Sven laughs, but it's an ominous laugh, promising more clouds to come, clouds bringing rain and thunder beyond compare.

"What do you want?" my father growls from the speakerphone.

I know that if he could, he would reach through the phone and grab this bastard by the throat, not letting go until the final breath finally escaped his wretched body. But, that is all wishful thinking. I remain here, handcuffed, with this crazy man whose intentions I still don't know.

"The thing you're hiding in your safe," Sven leans in all the way to the phone, hissing right into the speaker, as tiny droplets of his sweat squirt all over the surface of my phone.

"What thing!?" my father thunders. "What the Hell do you mean!?"

"I'm not prolonging this conversation any more than I need to," Sven replies shortly. "I'll call again in two hours, with clear directions on where to leave the stash. Oh, and remember one thing," Sven pauses for a moment, and his body slithers behind me, as his hand rests on the nape of my neck. He can probably feel my heartbeat, about to explode. "If I even smell the cops, I'll leave a trail of Maddie's parts, which you can follow back to me. I promise you that. Two hours, Hugo."

And, with those words, he grabs the phone and smashes it against the opposite wall. The phone bursts into a million tiny little pieces, which glimmer on the concrete floor, like tears. But, I'm not crying. I don't feel sad. I feel scared, petrified. My mother always taught me that crying when you're scared is the worst reaction you could have. It hinders rational thinking, which might prevent you from reaching a solution to your problem. And, seeing this man, he doesn't seem to be the type to fall for tears. It's a futile effort at nothing.

I watch the metallic phone parts sparkle for a moment longer, then Sven pulls me up.

"Let's go."

"Where are we going?"

He is more agitated now, pushing me towards the door forcefully, even though I've done everything he asked me to do. We continue towards the car in silence, and he shoves me into the backseat again. He himself sits on the driver's seat, grasping at the steering wheel hard.

"You better hope for your sake that your father brings me what I want," he hisses, as he looks at me through the rear view mirror. There is no more trace of that nice, polite guy from a few hours ago. This is the voice of a man who is no stranger to hurting women. Those are the eyes that have seen his own hands do horrendous things.

I just nod, lowering my head. Whatever he is asking, my father will give it to him. I'm sure of that. He was told not to contact the police, but what do people usually do under these circumstances? I remember all those kidnapping movies I've seen and getting the police involved never turns out the way everyone planned.

I hear the start of the engine, and we're back on the road. It's difficult to stay awake. I feel drugged, but I'm sure I wasn't. At least, not again. I didn't drink anything, and by this point, I'm becoming parched. But, I won't ask for anything from this man. Even if it's the last thing I do.

I clench my hands into fists, and subconsciously try to pull my hands apart, but that only tightens the metallic grip, which digs into my flesh, leaving bright red marks. My eyelids are becoming heavier and heavier, and soon, despite all odds, I drift into sleep again.

CHAPTER 4

Andersen

Of course Hugo had no other way but to call us. This is exactly what I told Fynn, when we got the call. It helps that we all go way back, but despite what people think, it's advisable to notify the police when someone has been kidnapped, and especially when there's been a ransom call.

"You think Sven's working alone?" Fynn asks me, downing his coffee. I always joke it's like him, black and bitter.

It always surprised me how easily he could eat and drink in the car. Like, he had some inner balance the rest of us didn't. He puts the paper cup in the pocket of the door.

"I doubt it," I reply, with my eyes firmly on the road. "Hugo knows it, too. That's why it's crucial that we find his daughter in the next hour or so. Sven's unpredictable, like a cat in a box. You open the lid and you don't know if the cat's gonna be sleeping or if it's waiting to claw your eyes out."

I swerve quickly to the left, and we both lean a little to the opposite side, then quickly regain our balance.

"We don't even know if the girl is still alive," he says.

"Don't let Hugo hear you talk like that."

"Shouldn't he know the odds?"

"You don't tell a father that his child might be dead," I give him a scornful eye, but he doesn't mind it, as usual.

"Come on, it's not like Hugo doesn't know Sven. The guy's an animal. He kills on instinct. Honestly, I'd be surprised if the girl is still alive and kicking," Fynn snorts, and I know there's no way prolonging this conversation. "But, you're free to have your la-di-da moment, thinking we'll swoop in and save the day."

"Don't we always?" I grin, stepping on the gas.

Fynn is right. I do want to arrive there and save the girl. Sven's a monster. I still remember the last time we had to clean up after him. The thought of that sight churns my stomach. But, he always manages to get away somehow. Well, not this time.

"Like I said, keep dreaming, Prince Charming."

With those words, we both stay silent for the rest of the journey. We reach the abandoned building easily. We find the broken phone inside. Fynn picks up the biggest piece, then smells it.

"They were here an hour ago."

"Can we track them?"

I sniff the air, but a childhood fire accident rendered my sense of smell almost non-existent. Still, I occasionally try, just for the heck of it. However, I get nothing.

I turn to Fynn. His nostrils are flaring, his lips are half parted. His pupils are widening, barely noticeably. He'll catch the scent. He always does. I follow him outside, and he stops on a small patch of gravel, surrounded by unmowed grass. It's the dead of night, but the tire tracks are clearly visible when Fynn flashes a light onto the ground.

"The girl left this place alive," he informs me, and a huge burden falls off my shoulders. But, that doesn't mean she'll arrive alive. Dammit. Fynn's negativity always tries to get to me.

Sometimes, it's hard to stay positive around him, but those of us who have gone through thick and thin with him, know this and accept this. I guess we all had some shit in our childhood that shaped us into the obnoxious men we are today. But, now's not the time to go down memory lane and plan on righting wrongs that may not even be made right. Now is the time to save a girl from a monster, like the story went in those good old fairy tales.

Fynn doesn't say anything else. He heads over to the car, and hops into the driver's seat. I ride shotgun this time. It's always faster that way. He knows where we're going, so it's easier to have him drive, rather than him giving me instructions.

The road we're taking is dark. The trees are looming over the narrow dirt road, and there is a sense of impending doom. That's at least, what I expect Fynn to say, to lighten up the mood, but he's silent, and that is the unsettling part. He usually has some snarky comment to make, expressing the worst case scenario, and how we should all be ready for it. But, there's none of that now. He is focused on the road; his hands are keeping a firm grasp on the steering wheel. Not even the radio is on.

"We getting close?" I ask, unable to stand the silence any longer.

Fynn doesn't reply immediately. Just nods a moment later.

"You think Sven's alone?" I ask again.

"Not unless he's the stupidest idiot I've ever met," Fynn replies. "And, we both know Sven. He's many things, and idiot isn't one of them."

Fynn's got a point. The last place was just a ruse. He took the girl there, knowing we'd be tailing him. This other location is where the showdown will take place. I can feel it in my bones, just like I can feel it that the girl is alive. She must be. Otherwise, Hugo won't be making the deal. Like Fynn said, Sven's no idiot. Keeping the girl alive is what keeps this exchange possible.

"What do you think he needs it for?" I ask once more, but this is more of a rhetorical question I'm asking myself.

Still, Fynn replies. "What do you think he needs it for?" Slightly cynical. Slightly making you feel like you should know better than ask such stupid questions. Classic Fynn.

"I'm surprised he even knows it's been in Hugo's possession all this time," I just continue, shrugging off his comment, which I've gotten used to. "I mean, we also didn't know it."

"We're small shits in the grand scheme of things," Fynn explains his view. "Only big players knew this info."

"Since when is Sven a big-time player?"

"Since he probably works for one."

And with that, I see Fynn turn left and park underneath a big, weeping willow tree, which hid us from plain sight. Making as little sound as possible, we get out of the car, crouching behind the tree. Fynn points at a nearby lodge. It looks abandoned, but not dilapidated. There are no cars around it. We see no people either.

"Is this really the place?" I make the mistake of asking this question.

Fynn just gives me a look that tells me all I need to know. If he says the girl is there, she's there. Dead or alive.

"So, how do we do this?" I whisper.

"Need to go around, see in the back," he replies, surveying the lodge. "The girl is here. Her scent is unmistakable. But, Sven knows how to mask his. So, all I can smell is her. Be ready for anything."

"Always am," I grin in the dark.

We do as he instructed. We check the back, and it all looks clear. I'm not sure which one of us is more confused, but we keep on going. We burst in through the back door, and the first thing we hear is whimpering coming from one of the corners. Fynn rushes over there, while I switch on the lights.

In one blazing moment, the inside of the lodge is lit up. It's just a single room, which functions as a kitchen, dining room, bedroom, all in one. My gaze wanders around it, until it finally lands on a young woman, tied up to a chair in the corner. Fynn's hands remove the ropes quickly, but the handcuffs on her hands are still there.

"Where are the keys?" he asks her, taking off the gag.

Her eyes are still adjusting to the light, bloodshot and red. Her hair is a mess of a bird's nest, and there are several scratches on her. But, apart from that, she's alive and well, which isn't what many who met Sven could boast with. This girl's pretty lucky.

"Let me do this."

I walk over to them, and I notice a hair pin in her hair. I reach for it, but the girl flinches, and scurries backward.

"I won't hurt you, I promise," I say this as soothingly as I can.

She opens her eyes again, so I reach for the pin and this time, she lets me have it.

"May I?"

I take her by the hands, and pick the lock on the handcuffs easily. One of my talents, I guess, if you could call it that. It's weird that a cop would know how to pick locks. But, it did come in handy more than once over the years of our service in the force.

"There," I take them off her cold, trembling hands. "Better?"

She nods. "T-thank you," she manages to muster.

"Are you alone?" Fynn asks, still on the lookout. It wouldn't be the first time someone jumped on us from the darkness, just as we were letting our guard down.

"The guy just... left," she says, not believing it herself. But, a few more seconds assured us that the inside of the lodge is safe.

"What the Hell, Sven?" Fynn grunts, resting his hands on his hips, and sniffing the air again.

"Are you alright?" I ask the girl. "Cold? Hungry? Thirsty?"

She rewards my efforts with a worn out smile. "A little thirsty."

"Let's get you back to the car, I have a bottle of water there and a blanket if you're cold."

She smiles even more widely at this, then follows me outside. I find the bottle in the glove compartment, and she drinks half of it thirstily. I also take out the blanket and wrap it over her shoulders, knowing it's not the cold that makes her tremble like that, but still, a warm sensation will relax her muscles.

"We'll get you back to your home in no time," I tell her. "Your father is eagerly waiting for your return."

"Did he send you?"

"Yes," I nod.

"So, you're the cops that the guy who kidnapped me clearly stated he doesn't want on the case?"

I can hear the brittle sharpness with which she cut me just now, but just like with Fynn, I choose to ignore it.

"This is a delicate situation, lady, and - "

"Don't call me lady, I have a name, you know."

"Miss Holloway, as I was saying, the guy who kidnapped you isn't just a small time crook, nor is the thing he asked for simple money. It's actually - "

"None of her business," Fynn appears, interrupting me curtly. "We're just here to get her home. Sven's not here anymore, so we can get the Hell out of here."

"But, why did he just leave me like that, after all that effort at getting me here?" the girl asks.

I look at Fynn, hoping he might have an answer to this, because I sure as Hell don't. This doesn't look like Sven at all. This is too calculated, like he's planned out 5 steps ahead, and is letting the situation unravel exactly according to his plan. That feeling doesn't sit right with me.

"Let us worry about that," Fynn chooses not to reply to that. "You just relax and you'll be home in no time."

The girl settles in the back of the car obediently. Her head rests on the back, and the slightly bumping motions of the car surging through unchartered paths outside the city finally make her drift off to sleep. I occasionally glance at her in the rearview mirror. She is breathing softly, barely visibly, her entire body wrapped up in the blanket I gave her. She looks like a little, lost lamb. More so than ever, I thank the Providence that we got this one back safe and sound.

I notice Fynn just stares at the road in front of us.

I don't like the look on his face. I don't like it at all.

CHAPTER 5

As we enter my father's study, he is sitting where he usually sits for important, possibly life-altering situations. I don't have to look at the heavy, crystal ashtray to know that there would be butts and ashes. His study looks smaller now, than it did before, when I was looking at it with a child's eyes. That big carpet on the floor has gotten a bit used up, as many shoes have crossed over it, some that would never step on it again. His library spanned all over one single wall, occupying the space from top to bottom. I remember leafing through them as a child, when he was in a good mood and allowed me to sit with him in here, on the condition that I didn't bug him. To my curious little brain, that was easy. I could have bugged him at any other time, but that was the only time when I could peruse all the books in his library, and even take one if I liked it enough to try and read it. Of course, most of it was dry economics, accounting and law related stuff, but in every row of books, there was one or two that didn't belong to any of these. He had The Malleus Maleficarum, translated as the Hammer of Witches. As a lonely child, I was interested in the uncanny, the unnatural and everything in between. So, this was the first book I took off his shelf. I still remember the feel of the old pages, as he managed to find an edition from about 100 years ago. I still remember that it was written by a Catholic clergyman by the name of Heinrich Kramer and that it was first published in 1486. He was pro killing witches and this was his goal in writing this book: a whole legal and theological theory regarding it.

As my dad's eyes raise to meet mine, I look to the side, straight to where the book is situated on his shelf. It's still there, in the same place where I left it 13 years ago.

My dad gets up and rushes over to me with arms stretched as wide as they go. He wraps me up in his bear hug, a strange but pleasant mixture of tobacco smells and warmth that emanates only from the realization that someone you thought might be dead wasn't really dead. I hug him back and bury my face in his neck. The two cops who brought me in give us a few moments.

When we finally separate, a little unwillingly though, my dad speaks to them.

"I really don't know how to thank you," his voice trembles, something I've rarely witnessed. Maybe only once in my entire life.

"We didn't do anything," the moody guy speaks first.

I have to admit I like the other one better. He at least asked me how I was doing and offered me a drink and his blanket. This guy barely looked at me. Not that I wanted him to look at me. But, if you come to rescue someone, don't you want to make sure they're alright when you actually find and rescue them?

"I wouldn't say that, Fynn," the other guy pats him on the shoulder, the way partners do. "We found her and brought her back safe and sound, didn't we?"

"She is back here because Sven arranged it that way," Fynn snorts, and again, doesn't even look at me. "He had it all planned out and we did exactly what he wanted us to do. Now, the question remains, why is she here, safe and sound, without him getting what he wanted?"

His voice lingers in the air, and I know my father is thinking about it. I myself am thinking about it. The guy just left me there, without a word. He threatened to kill me if he didn't get what he wanted, and he just left me. That can't be right. Even I know this much.

"Do you have it, Hugo?" Fynn asks.

"Of course," my father replies. "It's in my safe."

I wonder if it's in the safe everyone assumes he has, or in the other one, where he keeps the really valuable items. He doesn't elaborate, and neither do I.

"I was ready to hand it over for Maddie, like Sven asked."

"He's not working alone," Fynn says, what I know they're all thinking. "This is way too sophisticated for him. And, the ending is confusing as Hell. Why run without getting his hands on it?"

That curiosity catches my attention, and I wonder what it could be. I know my father has a few special items in his other safe, things that are better kept hidden than allowed to roam the world, getting transferred from one pair of wrong hands to another.

"That can mean only one thing," my father adds. "This is just the beginning. I'm sure that there's a phase 2 to whatever this is, and that'll be even more dangerous."

"Absolutely," the other cop finally chimes in. "That's why Fynn and I were thinking... you guys need to lay low for a while. We could arrange your stay at a safe house, and not even a battalion of tanks will be able to get through to you."

I see the look on my father's face change. He's remembered something, something that doesn't align well with this reasonable plan.

"I have to travel," he tells them.

"This is a little more important than your business, Hugo," Fynn eyes him scornfully.

"You don't understand. This is a multi-million dollar deal that's been planned for a year now. I can't back down. You don't understand the consequences this might have on my business. I... I just can't."

Listening to my father worry about his work when our lives were in danger hits a sore spot, but I know him. I know that he's built this company from ground up and I know how much it means to him. Giving in to that guy and whoever he's working with would be like giving up on everything he's worked for, losing his company, maybe even more. So, I can understand where he's coming from, even though Fynn doesn't seem to.

"I can hire bodyguards, pay them whatever to keep me safe," my father adds. "But, I need to be present at that meeting."

"Listen, Hugo - " Fynn starts but his partner interrupts him.

"Let's all calm down here," his voice is calm, friendly even. "If Hugo needs to go, then we can arrange for someone from our precinct to join him. Maybe, Rodnet and Kear."

"I don't know them," my father shakes his head.

"And, you don't need to," Fynn snorts again. "All you need to know is that they will keep you safe, at the expense of their own lives. So, if you really can't sit your ass down here and lay low, this is the only other option available."

"What about Maddie?" my father wonders, and I feel this is the first time Fynn actually looks at me, and not through me.

"She won't be going anywhere," Fynn shrugs. "It's difficult enough keeping an eye on one person who's got a target on his forehead, let alone two. And one of them being a girl who prefers bars."

"I beg your pardon!?" I take a step forward to him, ready to explain that the only reason I was at that bar was because my friends made me do it, and I was about to head home when all that happened.

"Alright, alright," my father lays his hand on my shoulder, trying to calm me down. "Fynn's a little rough on the edges, sweetheart. You'll get used to it. Just don't pay too much attention to what he says."

"Yeah, princess," Fynn grins at me, his ghostly white teeth, with fangs that I only noticed now. "If you want a shoulder to cry on, talk to Anderson there. But, if you want to stay alive, then do listen to what I have to say."

And, with those words, everyone is left speechless. The smirk on his face tells me he liked how that felt.

"So, Fynn and I were thinking," Anderson jumps in here, and we're all kinda happy he does, "we'll take Maddie to the safe house up North."

"Is that the one - "

"Yes," Anderson interrupts my father. "It's the one where we made sure that Milo would stay alive."

I have no idea what they're talking about, but I know it's important. I can't go back to my life knowing that the person who kidnapped me is still out there, maybe plotting something more, something worse.

"Take her there," my father agrees without another word said.

"What? Dad, I don't - "

"I can't stay here to keep you safe, sweetheart," my father tells me. "And, right now, these two guys are the only ones I trust. They're the only ones I know will be able to protect you."

Nothing else needs to be said. Nothing else needs to be explained. I know he's right. Especially if he's not here, I can't go back to my apartment alone. That guy probably knows all about where I live and that I'm alone there.

"When will you be back?" I ask him.

"I'll try to return as quickly as I can, hopefully a week, maybe two."

"As soon as your father returns, we'll take him to you," Anderson addresses me, and for some inexplicable reason, his words calm me. I trust him, even though I have very little to base that on.

"See?" my father joins in. "It'll be alright."

"I'd hate to cut this short, but we really need to get both of you out of here," Fynn tells us. "For all we know your house could be bugged, or under surveillance."

"I doubt that," my father shakes his head. "The bugged part, I mean. No one enters my study. I make sure to lock it when I'm not home. Not even the cleaning lady has access to it unless I'm here. So, if the place really is wired, this room would be the only safe one."

"If you say so," Fynn nods. "But that doesn't change the fact that we need to get out of here, now."

"Can I pack some stuff?" I ask.

"Come on, I'll walk you to your room, so you can grab what you need," Anderson tells me.

"No, my stuff is at my apartment."

"It's not safe to go there," Anderson tells me. "Do you have anything you can grab from here?"

"I guess."

"Let's meet up in front in 5 minutes," Fynn instructs, and Anderson nods.

We leave my father's study, and I start up the stairs first, but he grabs me by the elbow.

"Wait, I'll go first."

"You think someone's here?" The thought of there being an intruder who's just waiting to jump out from the darkness and kill us makes me shiver with fright. This has been one helluva night, and it looks like it's not nearly over.

"With the tight security Hugo has, it's doubtful," Anderson assures me, but something tells me he's only saying that to keep me calm. "But, seeing what you've been through tonight, it doesn't hurt to be extra careful."

"Thanks," I suddenly say. "For saving me, I mean. And, now for looking after me and my dad."

"Oh, it's fine," he flashes a row of pearly whites at me, as his disobedient curls fall over the left side of his face and right into his eyes. His shakes his head, then rakes his fingers through his hair, like a swim suit model. "It's all in a day's work."

"Well, still...." I smile.

"Don't worry," he tells me, sensing my fear, "everything will be alright."

I show him where my room is once we reach the top of the stairs, and he enters first. A few moments later, he returns and gestures me in.

"All clear," he announces.

I go in and grab my old backpack. Most of my stuff is in my apartment, but luckily I left some mostly unworn clothes here, which will do just fine under the circumstances. I stuff a few sweatshirts, a pair of sweatpants, some socks and underwear into my backpack, then turn to Anderson.

"All done?" he asks me. I nod. "That was quick."

"Not like I'm going on a holiday," I say a little more snarkily than I planned. "Sorry."

I immediately bite my lip. It's not his fault. And, he's been so kind and sympathetic, unlike his partner.

"It's OK," he assures me. "You've been through Hell tonight. You're allowed to snap."

"But, not at you. You're the least to blame for all this."

"Don't worry, I'm thick-skinned," he winks at me, and before he manages to turn around and exit the room first, my cheeks blush poppy red.

He shows me another smile, and politely chooses not to comment anything else. We both get out of the room, slowly descend the stairs and head out to the front door. This house, so vast and grand, looks like a trap from this perspective, and I always felt safe there. Funny how things change in a blink of an eye. But, if anyone should know that, it's me.

My dad and I get into the police car, and watch as the headlights disperse through the darkness in front of us, illuminating the way ahead.

The only question is will this light be enough to save us?

CHAPTER 6

After we drop my father off at the police station, and Fynn settles everything with the two cops that are going to keep my father safe during his business trip, we continue our way to the safe house. Fynn is driving, and looking at his profile image from the back seat, I can see the sharp outlines of his clenched jaw, the veins in his lower arms and hands jutting as he firmly grasps the steering wheel.

Anderson, on the other hand, seems jovial. If he feels any concern or fear about this whole thing, he's doing a great job of hiding it. Occasionally during the trip, I want to ask something, but I stop myself, because I'm worried Fynn might answer it first, and I don't really feel like talking to him. So, I remain quiet, and eventually doze off.

At some point later on, I'm woken up by someone's gentle nudge on the shoulder.

"Hey, Maddie?" The voice is soft, soothing, it almost blends into my dream. "Wake up, we're here."

The voice continues to stir me, and I finally open my eyes to find Anderson's face a few inches away from mine, his wide grin aimed straight at me. I clear my throat a little, as I pull back, afraid I'll blush again. He gets the hint and does the same. We're at a safer distance now, but his smile is still there. He offers me his hand, and I take it, exiting the car like royalty, but not really feeling like it.

"So, this will be home, sweet home for the next month or so," he says, as we both gaze at the inconspicuous looking house in front of us.

When they said a safe house, I guess my mind conjured up images of bars on the windows and alarms, and all those other things that are supposed to make a house safe, but I see this place has none of that. It's just a house, one you'd pass by without even checking out twice. Maybe, that's the whole point exactly.

"It's much better on the inside," Anderson adds, as if he senses my disappointment. "I know it's probably not what you're used to, but..."

"If it keeps me alive, then it's exactly what I'm looking for," I try a smile, and it works.

"Why are you standing here in plain sight? Get inside," Fynn pushes past us, separating me and Anderson as he does so.

Anderson pretends to roll his eyes, but there is still a smile on his face, and for some reason, I know that the relationship between these two is strong. It has gotten past those little insecurities people have, and they have obviously accepted each other, flaws and all. Not that it looks like Anderson has much of them. Pleasing on the eyes, charming, helpful, chatty. He's the exact opposite of Fynn.

Anderson gestures at me to go first this time. We walk up a small wooden patio, covered in splotches of darker paint. It creaks underneath the weight of our bodies. There are two rocking chairs, and a small table between them. I can't really see myself having my morning coffee here, but I understand the purpose behind this scene. It's supposed to convey an image of a house where the dwellers aren't afraid to sit outside and be seen by occasional passers-by. Not that there is much traffic around here. We were brought to this place by a small patch of dirt road, and I bet you can only find it if you know what you're looking for. Otherwise - good luck.

Fynn is already inside, so we follow him. When I enter, an unpleasant smell of a lack of usage hits my nostrils. I guess it shows on me, because Anderson immediately jumps to explain.

"Yeah, we definitely need to air the place a little," he winks at me, and I chuckle. Maybe it won't be so bad with him here.

Fynn walks out from the last room down the hallway. "Your room is that one." He points. "Anderson and I are sleeping in the room next to yours." I just nod. "The kitchen is to your left. You've got your basic utilities, but the coffee sucks. The machine has its own mind and will refuse to make you coffee occasionally. Apart from that, the toaster is working fine, and the microwave, too."

"So, we'll be cooking?" I wonder.

"We can't quite order out here, princess," he snorts at me.

"That's not what I meant," I reply.

"Cut her some slack, Fynn, will ya?" Anderson's soft voice tingles in my right ear, where he also places his hand upon my shoulder. "The girl's been through enough for one night."

"She will be through more if we aren't careful. Sven isn't finished with her, you know this yourself, Anderson."

"I know, but come on."

"You can be all freakin' lovey-dovey for all I care, but someone here needs to keep his head on his shoulders, if we're all gonna get out of this alive." With those words, he sighs, then shakes his head. "I'll go outside to check the premises. You can help her settle in."

"Fynn, I didn't mean - " Anderson starts, but Fynn is already out the door.

Now, it's Anderson turn to sigh, as he gestures helplessly at me.

"He's not really a bad guy."

"Yeah, he just sounds and acts that way," I furrow my brow.

"I know that's how it looks to you, and I'm pretty sure that's how it looks to most people. But, once you scratch that hard, edgy surface... trust me, there's no one else I'd rather have by my side when shit hits the fan."

"Like it did this time?"

"Well..." he scratches the back of his head, and gives me a mischievous, boyish look to die for.

"I'll take that as a yes," I chuckle. "So, you know this guy? This Sven?"

"Sort of," Anderson nods, walking around a small coffee table and sitting on the sofa. "We got unofficial records saying he's done everything under the sun, but we could ever only catch him on some minor stuff that would barely hold up in court. That, plus his lawyer is an unforgiving piranha, so we always need to do everything by the book, otherwise the evidence we get on him is deemed unacceptable in the court of law."

"Tough."

"Tell me about it," he sighs again. "Every time something big happens and we manage to connect it to him, he's nowhere to be seen. And, it's been a while since he's been active. Maybe even a few years. The fact that he's out of hiding, sort of, and pulling a stunt like this, kidnapping you, tells us more's at stake here. There are some big players involved, I'm sure of it."

"Big players? You mean, like my dad?"

"Even bigger."

"That's really big then. But, I don't understand, what does any of this have to do with my dad? And, what is it that Sven wanted? Why didn't he ask for money, like any normal kidnapper would?"

Anderson allows me a moment or two, before replying. He gazes at me deeply, his eyes the color of ashes and smoke dispersing in the wind. I could sense that there is an intense truth he wants me to know, but he's still not sure if he should tell me.

"Do you know where your father's wealth comes from?" he suddenly asks me the question. I've never asked myself, but simply took it for granted that my father earned it. All of it. But now, faced with this dilemma, I realize how childish my convictions have been.

"From his business?" I shrug. "It's been doing pretty well, I think."

"Sure, pretty well, but millions of dollars' worth well?"

"I don't know," I shrug again. "It's none of my business. I mean, I don't run it, he does. So, why would I know the inner workings?"

"I guess it's not really something you'd like to share," he says solemnly.

"Why?"

"This is not for me to tell you," he suddenly pulls back.

"Tell me what?" I take a step closer to him. "You can't throw this bomb on me, and then say oh no, can't tell you, sorry."

"Well, that's what I'm saying, sorry. I shouldn't have started this conversation. It's not my place to tell you such a thing."

"Well, can you tell me one thing then?"

"What?"

"Is my father the bad guy here?" My voice trembles as I ask this, the tears struggling to flood my face, but I'm not letting them.

Anderson takes my hand in his. It's warm and soft.

"No, Maddie, your father isn't a bad guy at all. In fact, he's one of the nicest guys I've met. He just... made some mistakes that came back to haunt him, more than once."

"Is this one of those times?"

"I'm afraid so."

I slump down onto the sofa next to him, feeling an invisible burden pressing hard on my chest, not showing chances of letting go any time soon.

"Your father loves you very much." His hand is still on mine, and I don't know what to focus on, his words or his gentle touch. "And, everything he ever did was for you and your mother. Never forget that."

"I won't," I smile, feeling the exhaustion of all the previous events finally catch up with me, threatening to shut me down completely.

"You just need a good night's rest, or in this case, a good day's rest. When you wake up, it'll all seem a little less scary."

"You're probably right. I just don't know how that will happen. It feels like nothing will ever be the same."

"I know that's how you feel, but that's just it. A feeling. It's not the way things really are. I read somewhere that we create our own reality. Sort of like, wishful thinking really is wishful thinking. You think positively, so you wish for it, and often, the Universe actually answers."

"You read that somewhere, huh?" I smile curiously.

"Well, not that I have that much time to read lately, but yeah. It's one of those things I read and it just stuck."

"I know that feeling. Lately, life has gotten so busy that I barely have time to pick up a book let alone actually enjoy an evening with it."

"Priorities."

"Of course. Books aren't priorities most of the time."

"But, they should be."

"Right?" I beam at him. "So, do we have any books around here?"

I look around, hopeful for some bookshelf with hidden gems, but I see nothing here.

"There's a small bookshelf in your room. Not sure what it has, though. I wasn't furnishing this place, so..."

"I'll make sure to check it out then."

"If you're lucky enough to find something, then this month will be your perfect opportunity to lay down, relax with a good book in one hand and some coffee in the other, while Fynn and I take care of business."

"You mean, if the machine spits it out, right?" I laugh, and he joins in.

"It better," he tells me.

"Well, alright then. I think I'll go take a shower, because I feel horrible."

"Well, you don't look horrible," he tells me quickly, then even more quickly adds. "You look fine. I mean, you look better than fine. Just, you look fine for someone who was held captive a few hours ago. I mean...."

"I know what you mean." A tidal wave of warmth and gratitude washes over me, as I beam with a strange sense of happiness at not only being alive, but being here. "And, thank you. For everything. Even if it is just you doing your job."

I get up first, and he does the same.

"Rest well," he suggests. "If you need us for anything, we're right here, 24/7."

"Thanks," I raise my hand a little awkwardly in a gesture of goodbye, then walk down the short hallway to my room.

When I enter, I immediately close the door. Two large windows overlook the forest around us, and I see the mountains in the distance. Well, if I need to run, I should make sure not to run in that direction. What's the point of escaping someone who wants to kill you, only to die of thirst or hunger or fall prey to some animal in the woods?

I put my backpack on the bed. It's covered with a woven blanket, the likes of which old Nordic grandmas would make for a newborn, all colorful and checkered. It makes me smile. That's the second thing around here that makes me feel welcome. Maybe this month won't be so bad, after all. That is, if I manage to avoid Fynn at all cost, which is not really possible. But, I can at least try. He obviously doesn't want to be here. I'm sure Anderson doesn't either, but at least he's being nice about it. Not like I asked them both to be here and babysit me. I sigh, realizing that such thoughts aren't really helpful.

I see a door in the corner, and upon opening it, smile at the fact that I have my own bathroom. It's small, and once inside, I can't spread my arms to the side. The shower stall is inconvenient and I'll probably hit my elbows against the walls all the time. I have to lean to the side while sitting on the toilet, not to hit the sink with my shoulder or head. But, at least it's some privacy, and under these conditions, I'll gladly take it.

I grab a t-shirt and a clean pair of undies from the backpack, then jump into the shower. It's like I thought. I can barely turn around, but I manage it somehow. When I get out, I see a clean toothbrush and toothpaste on the sink. So, they really have thought of everything. I brush my teeth, and go under the blankets. I consider closing the curtains, but the view is too beautiful. The mountains are majestic, covered in lush greenery and I can't stop staring at them.

Slowly, without me even realizing, I drift off into deep sleep. The fear stops looping at some point, and my thoughts become a car burning up the road, smoothly taking over hills and valleys, heading into the warm, sunny horizon.

CHAPTER 7

F^{ynn}
     I check the perimeter quickly. This is definitely easier done in the daytime. And, even the woods surrounding us don't seem so dark and ominous, as they usually do. Still close to the house, I pause. I listen. The sound of my own footsteps is silent. I hear only the wind. Usually, the wind is my friend. My sense of smell is unbeatable, and the wind usually knows to escort anything important my way.

Suddenly, a flutter of leaves is raised off the ground, swirled in the wind, and then smashed against the ground. Rain's coming. The leaves are like eyes, staring at me.

Whatcha gonna do, Fynn? Ya gonna lose this one, like ya lost the other one?

The words flooded my ears. I could hear all those ancient voices buried deep inside my mind, reminding me that I failed. Telling me I would fail all over again. Hoping I would fail all over again.

I rub my eyes, opening them. There's a cage all around us. I can smell it. The bars are closing in, and we don't even see it. I can't blame Anderson. It's just how he is. He's an upbeat guy. You can beat him, but you can't break him. The more you block his sunlight, the more he convinces you he's a rain kinda guy and never needed the sun in the first place.

Not me. You can't beat me, and you sure as Hell can't break me. You can't break something that's already been broken. It doesn't work twice. That's what makes me a good cop. I don't get distracted. Never again. I made that mistake once, and it cost me half of my life. The other half I'm left with is barely good for anything. But, I keep pushing on. What else is there to do?

I walk back towards the house, and just as I'm about to open the front door, I hesitate. I remember what Anderson said. The girl probably doesn't want to see me, even in passing. It's good Anderson's here. He'll know how to handle her.

I turn to the wicker chairs on the patio and collapse into one of them. I hear it squeal underneath my weight, but eventually it settles in. At that moment, Anderson comes outside. He takes the other chair. He puts two beers on the table. Opened, of course. No glasses. That just means washing up.

"How is she?" I ask, reaching out for the bottle closest to me.

"What do you think?" He shrugs.

"If I knew I wouldn't be asking," I snort. I do that too much, I know. But, it's hard to fight an instinctual response.

"Well, you could have asked her that yourself, you know," Anderson tells me and I know he means well.

"She's unstable."

"No, you're just an asshole."

"Point taken," I nod, as we clink beers. "So, how is she?"

"I wouldn't say she's unstable. Considering everything, she's... fine. Worried about what might happen, of course, but that's a given. She's a sweet girl. You should actually try talking to her."

"I think I'll leave the consolation part to you," I sneer. "You seem to be doing it well."

"You don't think that I - "

"I don't think anything," I shake my head defensively. "She feels safer with you. I'm fine with that. You can be the inside guy, and I'll just be the watchdog."

"As always?" Anderson cheers again, and we both take a long sip from our beer bottles. "Go inside to rest. I'll take the first shift."

"You sure?"

"Yeah. You'll get the night shift, so I'm actually being selfish here," he chuckles.

"You sly dog," I laugh as well.

I finish the rest of my beer, then head on inside. As I pass the girl's door, it's tightly shut. No sound can be heard from inside. She smells of apple orchards in the spring, but the path there is closed. Trespassers aren't allowed, and that's probably what I'll continue to be. That doesn't matter. What matters is that she comes out of this alive and unharmed.

CHAPTER 8

I have no idea how much I've slept when I wake up, it's still daytime. I check my watch, and it has been only a few hours. Yet, I feel strangely well rested. That's stress and adrenaline for ya. Receive the right mixture of the two components, and you've got a helluva cocktail.

I get up, and dizziness hits me. I stop, mid-motion, allow my head to adjust to the newly awake sensation, then get up completely, with both feet on the ground. One sniff in the wrong direction and I realize that I need another shower, even though I did take one before I went to sleep.

One quick shower later and I feel better, almost fine, actually. This realization surprises me. This is my first official day in this safe house, not counting the day of the arrival, and for some reason, I want to start it the right way, whatever that means in this instance. I put on a loose sweatshirt on top, and a pair of leggings, and walk into the kitchen, which smells pleasantly of pancakes.

There, I see Anderson by the stove, with a big plate of pancakes sitting on the counter next to him. He is humming a tune I don't recognize, as he skillfully flips the pancake in the air.

"And, voila!" he shouts at no one really, as he successfully flipped the pancake over in the air, allowing it to fall gently back into the pan.

I chuckle loudly, and at that moment, he turns around. If I didn't know any better, I'd think he blushed a little.

"Oh, hey!" It only takes him a moment to regain composure and be his charming, assured self. "Didn't see you there."

"I noticed," I smile. "Nice flipping, by the way."

"Oh, that," he grins. "Just something to pass the time. You'll see, staying in a safe house isn't all fun and games."

"Oh, really?" I smirk. "And, here I am, thinking we'll be having non-stop parties. I mean, that's what your partner seems to think."

His face immediately changes at the mention of his partner. "Seriously, don't take everything Fynn says to heart. His tongue is faster than his brain and he often says things he doesn't mean."

"He sure sounds like he means it." I take a seat at the kitchen table, and eye those pancakes. "But, I'd rather have some breakfast first, and then discuss the unpleasantries of our stay here."

I see him trying to suppress a smile, but he can't. He adds the last pancake to the tower of others, and puts the pan away.

"There, I made us all breakfast," he announces. "We got maple syrup, some jam, honey, and powdered sugar."

"Sounds great."

He places the full plate in the middle of the kitchen table, then sets the tableware for me. I patiently watch him do it, as he swirls around, not once removing that grin from his face. It's pleasant, but almost feels a little strange. This is what my girlfriends told me that the morning after with a nice guy looks like. He's happy you're still there, and he'll gladly make you some breakfast before you leave.

The thought of having a one night stand has always been a conflicting one for me. It's not that I have anything against that. It's all about instant gratification, and if both parties agree to it, then by all means. But, I guess for me, sex has always been something intimate, something I wouldn't do with strangers. That's probably why I've only slept with one guy, and that was my high school sweetheart, with whom I was in a 5 year relationship. My girlfriends still make fun of me, occasionally nicknaming me the nun, but I know they don't mean anything bad by it. They understand it's just how I'm wired, and there's little I can do about it.

Anderson puts two pancakes on my plate, then tries to give me a third one.

"No, no," I shake my head. "I can't eat that much."

"Don't tell me you're on a diet?"

"No, just... three is too much."

"Since when are three pancakes too much for a grown up person?" He tilts his head a little to the side, to give me a weird, puppy dog eye look.

"It's not, I guess. I'm just not very hungry."

That seems to dissuade him, and he puts the third pancake on his own plate.

"Where's Fynn?" I ask, but not out of any desire to see him. Still, my question surprises Anderson.

"On the porch," he explains. "Someone always needs to be on the lookout. Especially at night."

"Is that how it always goes? This safe house deal, I mean."

"Yeah," he nods, pouring some maple syrup over his four pancakes. "But, with Sven, I'm surprised our chief didn't let us take some more guys."

His comment makes me put down my fork.

"I don't mean to scare you, but it's good for you to be aware of the situation," his voice is grave, but not hopeless.

"That's fine," I nod. "I don't want you to keep me in the dark."

"We don't plan on doing any such thing," he assures me. "Especially not Fynn. Only, he's doing it in his own, special way."

Our conversation takes on lighter overtones, and I feel pleasant again, almost completely safe, like my life wasn't hanging on the line.

"So, isn't he having any breakfast?" I ask, finally putting that piece hanging from my fork into my mouth.

The moment my tongue feels the sensation of taste, I realize that I'm starving. Maybe I really will have that third pancake, as the adrenaline has finally left my body, and now it is starving for nourishment.

"I told him to come, but I guess he's not hungry," Anderson tells me, not looking particularly concerned whether his partner will eat or not.

His face looks jovial, as he keeps stuffing it with maple syrup pancakes, but my mother's voice arises from somewhere deep inside of me and takes over.

"I can take some to him, outside."

My statement surprises us both. He starts coughing so hard, that I jump up and slap him on the shoulder, until he finally manages to breathe again.

"You OK?" I ask, my hand still electrified on his shoulder. I quickly pull it away, before he notices.

"Yeah..." he coughs again. "Fine. Thanks." He pauses, then nods. "Sure, take him some. He might... be hungry."

For some reason, I wonder if that's what he wanted to say initially, but I leave it alone. Instead, I put three pancakes on another plate, douse them with some maple syrup and then head outside.

I find Fynn sitting on the porch, in one of the rocking chairs. I feel like I'm seeing him for the first time now, when neither of us is veiled by darkness or fear. We're just two normal people, put in an abnormal situation.

"Hey," I tell him.

He just looks up at me. His piercing gaze confuses me. He has the look of a vet who's seen his fair share of human malice, and he'd rather just be left out of it all. I think he wants his eyes to appear fearsome, to make you think that he could hurt you just like that, so you'd better leave him alone, but in fact, they look sad. Deeply, profoundly sad.

"I thought you might like some food."

I put the plate on the table to his side. He just glances at it, but doesn't say anything. He doesn't reach for them. He doesn't say thank you. His eyes have already switched back to looking into the distance, expecting to see something before anyone else does.

"Well, ok then," I say, feeling more awkward than ever. "I guess I'll go back inside."

His eyes don't move. I turn away from him, and the moment I touch the door to push it open, I hear his voice.

"Thank you."

I acknowledge it with a barely visible nod, and a smile that belongs only to me. I return to the kitchen, and see that Anderson has finished with his food and has already washed his plate.

"Coffee?" he asks, drying his wet hands on a kitchen towel.

"Sure," I nod, sitting back down.

"I'm afraid we don't have milk, but we do have some creamer."

"That's fine."

I see him hovering over a small, vintage looking coffee machine that chortles out a small coffee in one big splat. He puts it carefully before me, then hands me the creamer.

"Let's see if it thinks I deserve a coffee as well," he chuckles, but as soon as he presses the same button as before, nothing happens. He tries a few more times, but doing the same thing over and over again rarely produces different results. "Stupid son a bitch machine..." he whispers to himself, but I hear him loud and clear.

His curse attack makes me laugh, and it feels good, like I haven't laughed in a long time.

"Sorry," he tells me, gesturing at himself helplessly. "I can be pretty crude sometimes."

"You're fine," I assure him.

"Can I get you anything else?"

"A glass of water maybe?"

"Coming right up," he lifts his index finger in the air, like a superhero wannabe, then turns over to the bottles of water and pours some into a glass for me.

But, before he can set it down nicely on the table, he trips over something on the small carpet, and the glass, along with all the water inside, end up on my sweatshirt. I jump, squawking at the cold sensation that washes over me in an instant, jumping up from my seat.

"Oh, crap..." he manages to muster. "I'm so sorry..."

"It's fine - " I start, but before I can say anything else, I feel his hands pressing the kitchen towel onto my breasts, which are tightly pressed against the thin fabric of the sweatshirt. It is only now that I realize I'm not wearing a bra, which isn't advisable if you're going to be entering a wet t-shirt contest.

Mortified as well as amused, thinking what my girlfriends would say if they saw me like this, with a guy dabbing my wet chest with a kitchen towel, I can't even move. It takes him a moment longer to realize what he's doing, and he immediately stops.

"Oh, I just made it even weirder, didn't I?"

He looks at my breasts, then realizes he's not looking where he's supposed to be looking, so he quickly lifts his glance up to the level of my eyes. At this point, neither of us can resist laughing, so we both start cracking up. I've totally forgotten all about my nipples poking through my sweatshirts, and I just laugh jovially, heartfelt and without restraint.

At some point, I finally remember to cross my hands in front of my chest, and nod, not really knowing what else to do.

"I guess I'll just go and change," I say, blushing more than ever, but somehow, not caring.

"Again, I'm so sorry," he repeats, making sure to keep his eyes firmly upon mine, not straying for a single moment. "It wasn't intentional..."

"Relax, it's fine," I smile, still nodding, feeling like a bobble head, but unable to stop the motion. "I'll just..." I point at the hallway. "I'll be right back..."

I run into my room to hide, feeling like this house's been struck by the latest Ice Age, and my nipples had a lot to say about it. Now, I could start overthinking this, and being embarrassed, but seeing I need to spend a whole month here, with Anderson under the same roof, maybe overthinking wasn't the right way to go.

"Just... let it go," I whisper to myself, my eyes closed.

As I exhale deeply, I change into another sweatshirt, making sure to put on a bra underneath, this time. We all know lightning rarely strikes twice in the same place, but you can never be sure. I return to the kitchen shortly, and see Anderson has cleaned up the table and all the dishes are already done.

"Wow," I smile. "It's like having a maid."

He chuckles. "You didn't think you'd be doing any cleaning while here, did you?"

"Well, why not?" I sit down opposite him, grateful that we've already moved past the awkward episode and we can chat nicely again. "You guys are supposed to keep me safe, but I don't remember anyone mentioning you guys cleaning up after me."

"Well, ask Fynn and you might get a different answer," he shrugs, with a wink, "but, I think it's nice to do these little things. I mean, it's just a few dishes. I don't mind washing them, instead of leaving them in the sink to dry up and then, it's Hell washing up."

"Spoken like a true housewife," I can't help but giggle.

"Keep talking like that, and you'll be doing your own dishes," he jokingly threatens me with his index finger.

"Alright, alright," I surrender, in good humor.

"So, have you managed to find anything good on your bookshelf?"

"I haven't even checked, sorry."

"No need to apologize," he smiles.

"I'll take a look as soon as I - "

The sound of approaching footsteps makes us both look in the direction of the front door, where Fynn immediately appears.

"Everything good?" Anderson asks.

"Yes," Fynn nods, giving me a skimming look, then placing his empty plate on the table before us. "Your turn to watch."

"Alright then."

With those words, Anderson stands up. "If you try to make a coffee later on, see if the old girl will make one for me, too," he tells me.

"Sure," I nod, with a smile.

Fynn doesn't say anything else. He just heads to their room, closing the door behind him. With both of them gone in their opposite directions, I am left alone. I'd love to talk to my friends, just to see how they're doing, only to hear their voices, but I know that's impossible. So, I head back to my room, to check that bookshelf, even though I myself have already started feeling like I'm in a novel of my very own, and the end was still very much a mystery to every character involved.

CHAPTER 9

Anderson
I exit into the fresh air, exhaling loudly. I remember the little tap which draws water from a nearby well, and I head over there. The splash of cool water on my face feels restoring. I'm not sleepy or tired. It's the opposite, actually. I'm too spirited, I guess is the word. Way too spirited than I should be, under these unwelcoming circumstances, but it is, what it is.

Bouncy. Peppy. Zesty. I think of all those terms my mom used to refer to when she'd be talking about boys and their strayed thinking when it came to girls. I guess that's exactly how I feel now. The sight of Maddie's nipples piercing through the light fabric of her sweatshirt still returns to me. Actually, I can't say that it returns, because it never left me. So, it's stayed with me since I first laid eyes on them. And, the image is still as fresh in my mind as half an hour ago.

I splash some more water on my face and for a moment, I feel refreshed. But, the image returns again, with a vengeance. I feel a stirring in my pants, something that has no place happening here or now. I can't think that way about her. Maybe Fynn is right. I'm way too friendly sometimes, and occasionally, it came back to bite me in the ass. I don't want that to happen now. I can't lose focus of what's important here, and that's Maddie's safety. I can't go around with a freakin' boner, wondering how it would feel to fuck her brains out. Fynn would kill me. Hugo would hang me by the balls. I know all that, and more. And, yet, her sweet face won't leave me, even when she's not around.

I sigh heavily, knowing that I need to work on this every single waking moment of my time here. That only adds more strain to the situation. But, it is what it is. I need to make it work somehow, and just keep my distance from her. That's the only way.

At that moment, I feel my work phone vibrating. It's a burner, specially bought for the purposes of coming here, and it'll only be used for a few days. Then, either Fynn or I will go and get another one, for the next few days. We can't risk being tracked this way.

"Hello?" I pick up, already guessing who will be on the other end of the line.

"Anderson?"

"Yes, Chief Garth?"

"Have you settled in?"

"Everything according to plan so far, Sir."

"I'm glad to hear that," he pauses a little, which worries me. He usually speaks in one elongated sentence which more resembles a monologue than a dialogue, and all you are left with is to simply agree. "Listen, I will need you to come down to the station tomorrow."

"Tomorrow?" I repeat, stunned. "But, you know that means leaving Fynn alone with the girl?"

"I am fully aware of that fact, Anderson, and believe me, I wouldn't ask you if it wasn't a matter of great urgency. But, it is. We need you down here for a few hours."

"Well, if it's an urgent matter..."

I lift my gaze up to the sky. The clouds are grey, promising the arrival of rain. So, it won't be the usual quick ride. I'll have to drive slower.

"It concerns one of your previous cases, the Higgins drowning."

He knows he doesn't need to say anything more. It was the case that Fynn and I couldn't crack for years. A young girl drowned, and everything kept pointing out to an accident. But, something just didn't sit right. The girl was a good swimmer, plus she knew those waters. She had lived close to the lake since she was born, and knew not to go in from the side where she was found. After much digging and poking around, after stepping on many corns, we discovered that her ex-boyfriend dragged her into the water by the hair and kept pushing her under the surface, until she was finally gone. Those bruises on her body fit perfectly with that story. Everyone always assumed that they were made post mortem, as her body lay there in the shallows, subject to the weather and rough rocks. Long story short, we couldn't help the girl, but at least we had him. And, having him in the interrogation room was one of the rare times I almost lost it. The whole thing is still a blur to me, but I remember my hands around his neck and others me pulling off of him. It was tough, but they erased it from the official record. After all, who's gonna believe a guy who murdered his ex in cold blood?

I still get the goosebumps when I remember that. I guess some things stay with you and never let you go, no matter how much you'd like them to. The only thing you can do is learn to live with it and if possible, learn from it. I learned that two wrongs don't make a right. As for Fynn, he learned his lesson some other time. More than once, actually.

"It's finally going to court and the DA wants to go over some things with you for the court hearing the day after tomorrow."

"Alright. I'll be there tomorrow," I tell him, squeezing the phone.

I don't want to leave Maddie and Fynn alone, but something tells me if I don't speak with the DA, the guy might walk. And, I'll be damned if that happens.

"Good. Keep me updated."

"Will do, Sir."

And, with those words, the chief hangs up. The idea of returning to a case I consider solved doesn't appeal to me, but I know the chief wouldn't call me back for nothing. Fynn will have to make by for a day. I'll try to wrap it up as quickly as I can and then, return. But, still, the thought of leaving Fynn without a backup doesn't sit right.

I return inside, and pass by Maddie's closed door. I continue to our room, and open without knocking. Fynn is in bed, but he's still dressed, staring at the window. When he sees me come inside, his whole body unwinds. It reminds me of being a boy and fearing my mom would walk in on me jerking off. Only, Fynn doesn't have that look on his face, that embarrassment. It's something else. Something much more sinister.

"Is everything OK?" he asks, immediately getting up, with his feet on the floor.

"No, no," I shake my head. "I mean, yeah, it's fine, don't get up..."

"Why aren't you out?" His voice is stern, but not agitated.

"The chief called."

"And?"

"I need to get back to the station tomorrow."

"For how long?"

"Just a day. Apparently, I have a meeting with the DA about the Higgins drowning."

"Oh," he nods.

"Will you be alright?" I ask, but I already know what he's going to say.

"Why wouldn't we be?" His answer is quick, cuts at the root. I'm used to it. But, I still ask.

"Well, not like I wanna go. But, it's important."

"Of course it is. I don't see why you feel the need to apologize for something that needs to be done."

After all these years, he still knows how to make me feel a little awkward, a little ridiculous, but I wouldn't trade this son of a gun for anything.

"Did you hear an apology come out of this mouth?" I ask, the tone turning into a joke, and we both jump on the bandwagon. "No. So, get your ass to bed, so you can be well rested tomorrow. You'll be keeping an eye on this place all on your own."

"You sure you don't want to take a nap?"

"Already did. I'm fine now. I'll take the next shift, and then head back. Hopefully, I won't be missing for more than a day."

"I've been awake longer than that," he snorts, good-humoredly.

"Yeah, but how well can you focus, after you haven't slept for a day?"

"Point taken," he chuckles. "Alright then. Get out of my sight now. How do you expect me to sleep with you constantly jabbering?"

"I'm gone, man, gone," I raise my hands in a gesture of surrender. "See ya before I go."

"Sure."

With those words, I close the door to our room, and walk back outside. The air is crisp, clean, as mountain air ought to be. As I take a walk off the porch and towards the unbeaten path, I feel like the earth has a pulse, which shoots through the ground, through the woods, all the way up to the mountains. I see all that lush greenery, and I can't feel any of the discord I'm usually a victim to back in the city. I try not to dwell on it too much, as it's too overbearing and drains energy, but sometimes, I grow tired of people's power over me, or the power they think they have over me. Their rules and regulations are too much, but I know that if we didn't have those, there would be total anarchy, and people like Sven would think they own the place. Can't have that. No way.

But, being here and now, I can enjoy the solitude of the mountains, and be the silent, almost ghost-like observer of the slow, almost impenetrable passage of time. As that great mountain in the distance looms over us, I know what the future brings. I can't keep hiding from it. The idea is instilled in my mind, as it is in my loins, and I know we must do something about it, otherwise we shall face extinction.

The greens around me lie in invisible jagged crevices, and the brilliant white of the sky is scorched by the oncoming clouds. The fangs of the future threaten to bite us all unless we find that someone. And, fast.

With those thoughts, I return to the porch. I remember one of the sayings my father used to repeat to us, on coming from his AA meetings. Yesterday's history, tomorrow's a mystery.

CHAPTER 10

It takes my body some time to adjust to the new sleeping arrangement, as well as the new bed. I wake up, quickly do my business in the bathroom, and then head out into the living room. There is of course, no Internet reception, but at least there is a TV, old fashioned and of questionable functionality, but I decide to give it a shot. I blow some dust from the DVD player cover, and check my choices. A few comedies, two horrors (no, thank you - I had more than enough horror in the last 2 days or so to last me a lifetime), some romance, some drama. I snort. I guess a comedy will do. I opt for Dr. Doolittle and his animal shenanigans, as I get comfortable on the bed.

Suddenly, I hear the sound of a car turned on. I jump from the sofa and rush outside. What awaits me is Fynn seeing off Anderson in the car which was already disappearing into the distance.

"Where's he going?" I muster, still looking after the car, feeling like a puppy whose owners decided to move but left it behind.

"He needs to head back," Fynn retorts.

"Why?"

He gives me a look as if trying to put me in my place, like I shouldn't even be asking such a question. Well, tough luck. I am.

"Police business."

He turns around and heads back into the house. I can feel that slow but steady burn of vexation rising from deep inside of me, and I know I won't just let this one go. I don't have Anderson now to be the buffer between us, so I need to show him that we're on the same side here, and there's no point in such animosity.

I rush in, after him, and catch him in the kitchen, getting himself a glass of water. With his back still turned away from me, facing the sink,

I stand in the middle of the kitchen, trying to come up with the best start to this awkward and unpleasant situation.

"Why do you hate me so much?"

This definitely wasn't what I intended to start with, but the little girl in me won over. She just wanted to know what was it that she did, which had such an effect on this man. Did she step on his little toe somehow? Did she insult him in any way? The poor thing had no idea.

I say this loudly enough for him to hear it, but he doesn't turn around. He downs his glass of water, then puts it on the kitchen counter. Then, slowly, he turns to face me.

"I don't hate you," he says simply. "What you seem to be forgetting is that we're not here to have fun. We're not here to watch movies and make popcorn. There is real danger out there."

"Don't you think I know that?" I snort back angrily. "I was face to face with this guy and trust me, I felt the evil steaming off of him, like some stench, which I doubt I'd ever be able to get rid of. So, believe me when I tell you that I know the danger we're in. Actually, the danger I'm in. Because, if for some reason we all separate, you guys will be just fine. You'll be able to take care of yourself. But me... not so much." I finally take a deep breath after this loud, angry monologue, feeling my chest burning on the inside. "Is it so wrong to ask for some decency when addressing me? Is that really too much to ask?"

I realize that neither of us feels like they're completely right, or completely wrong for that matter. We both stare at the floor in silence for a few moments, caught off guard by this moment of unexpected intimacy.

"I'm sorry," I finally say. "I know this is just a job for you, and we probably don't even have anything in common to be able to chat about. I guess I just took it too personally. I'll keep my distance from now on, and hopefully, this month will pass quickly, so we'll all be back to our lives..."

With those words, I turn to go, but his voice stops me.

"Wait...." he whispers, but I hear him. The word is followed by a heavy sigh, one I myself have released on more than one occasion.

I turn to him, more hopeful than I dare to be.

"There is no other way but to take this kind of a job personally."

"What do you mean?" I ask, confused, but strangely exuberant that we're actually talking, and not avoiding each other.

"Didn't Anderson tell you already?"

"Tell me what?"

"He usually has a big mouth," Fynn manages a smile, and his entire face lights up, making him look at least ten years younger. "I'm surprised he didn't explain my behavior."

"Well, he actually did mention something, that you have a reason to feel this way, but he didn't elaborate."

"Yeah, he just picks at the wound then leaves it open for someone else to close," he rolls his eyes, but I sense he means nothing bad by it. "I guess I might as well tell you what happened. Then, you'll see this isn't anything personal."

I sit down at the kitchen table, and he does the same. He rests his elbows on the table, his sleeves rolled up. I notice a few scars on his lower arms, deep and healed, but they would probably never disappear. I wonder who or what made them, but he starts his story and I focus on his words instead.

"A while back, Anderson and I were sent on a similar job, just like this one. The girl... Reba... we knew her from before. She was a childhood friend, and I guess you could say even more than that, a childhood sweetheart. We lost touch as adults, but this job and her needing protection brought us back together. It was like everything lit up again, I couldn't take my eyes off of her. Anderson went out one night, to get supplies, as we needed to stay hidden longer than we initially thought, so Reba and I remained alone at the safe house. I don't know how, but one thing led to another, and we ended up... well, doing what no one should be doing under those circumstances. We had no idea we were being watched, and after it, I guess I fell asleep. I just remember her arms around me, and me drifting off to sleep. What I woke up to was her dead body lying next to me, with a note crumpled up in her left hand."

"What did it say?" I whisper, not sure if I should say anything, but I couldn't keep quiet.

"Stay awake next time."

"Was it - "

"Sven, yes." He sighed sadly, deeply. "So, you see he was mocking me. But, that didn't matter. What mattered was that he was right. Reba's blood was on my hands. I should have kept her safe, and I failed to do that. I'm just wondering why they hadn't killed me as well. They could have easily."

I knew why they didn't, but I doubted he wanted to hear that, especially now.

"That's why I can't relax," he finally explains. "I can't be like Anderson. I can't chat about unimportant things, because I'm afraid that I'll relax too much, and I won't be on guard anymore. I can't lose anyone else."

"I trust you," I tell him softly, surprised by my own words.

The realization of what he just told me touched my heart. He was responsible for someone dying. I couldn't even imagine how that must feel, how it must keep him up at night. The sight of someone's lifeless body next to you, someone whose life you were supposed to save. I shudder at the thought of knowing what that feels like.

"You should only trust yourself," he corrects me. "Because, one way or another, we are all alone. We are born alone, we die alone, and occasionally, someone comes along, who might make that loneliness a little less tangible. But, life is one big solitude."

"That's a sad way of looking at things."

"Sad or not, that way of thinking keeps you alive."

"But, just because we talk about something in a nice way, doesn't mean that we're not being careful."

"We're being reckless. Our guard is down. We're focusing on something else, something that isn't a priority. We're getting closer to each other, and that's never a good thing under these circumstances."

It saddens me to think this way, but I understand where he is coming from. He doesn't want to get close to me, to anyone really, and I can't blame him. But, at least, it's good to know that it's nothing personal. I haven't done anything to cross him.

"I understand," I smile. "I'll let you do your job from now on, and I won't be a nuisance."

"I never said you were a nuisance," his voice made me blush. "Just stop thinking I hate you. Please."

"Deal," I grin.

"Well, alright then, if everything is OK now, I guess I'll go out on the porch, and just watch. Anderson should be coming later in the afternoon, maybe even in the evening. Do you need him to get you something while he's in the city?"

"No, I'm good," I nod. "But, thank you."

He nods, with his lips pressed tightly together. I still can't read him. At least, not like I can read Anderson. But, scratching on the surface of this reclusive man has brought me unexpected pleasure. Like he is a box that needs to be kept closed all the time, otherwise both good and bad things might come out of it.

As I watch him close the front door, I wonder what would happen if that box were to open. Would it frighten me? Or, would I welcome what comes with open arms?

Chapter 11

Early in the evening, I hear the same sound of the car once more, but I don't rush outside. I'm still in my bed, reading my book. My legs are tingling. They want me to run into the kitchen, and start a conversation with Anderson. I want to ask him what he's been up to. I want to see him smile, and tell me again that I shouldn't worry about anything. But, I remember Fynn's words. We shouldn't get close to one another. None of us. We need to stay on our toes. We need to focus on the fact that this isn't a vacation. He said so himself. We're in danger, at any waking moment, and we shouldn't do anything that prevents us from focusing on that.

I'm still holding the book in my hands, but I can barely focus on the plot and what the protagonist is going to do next. I couldn't care less. My ears are pricked up, focusing on even the slightest noise coming from the outer side of my closed doors. Suddenly, I feel thirsty and I see that the little pitcher of water by my bedside is empty. I get up, without thinking and grab it, walking to the kitchen.

Anderson is already there. He hasn't even taken his jacket off yet. There's a big, brown paper bag on the counter, overspilling with greenery and colorful bags.

"I know you guys didn't say to get anything, but I figured we could do with some chips and salsa," he grins at me.

"You're reading my mind," I say.

"I did get some fruits and vegetables, too," he adds, defensively. "So, you don't tell Hugo that we fed you only shit."

I chuckle. "Your secret is safe with me."

He starts taking out all the food and places it carefully in the pantry, and the fridge.

"Everything was good today?" he suddenly asks me.

"Yeah," I nod. "Why?"

"Well..." He rakes his fingers through his hair, leaving half of the paper bag still full of food. "You were alone with Fynn, and last time we spoke, I didn't get the impression you liked him all that much."

"Yeah, that was exactly the impression I had about him," I smile. "But, we talked. Really talked. And, I understand where he's coming from."

"You do?" My confession catches him off guard.

"He told me about... Reba? I think that was her name."

"He actually told you that?"

"Yeah."

"Wow," Anderson seems shocked. "He doesn't really talk about it, unless he really has to."

"Well, I didn't push him or anything..."

"Oh, I'm sure you didn't. But, I'm just surprised that he'd open up to someone like that, someone he doesn't know." Then, he adds, with a little smile on his face. "I think you two have a positive effect on each other."

"Positive?"

"Absolutely," he nods. "It's just that neither of you knows it yet."

"I mean, I'm happy that we've cleared up the air and all, but I don't really see us having much in common."

"Well, you never know."

"I doubt I'd ever find out, to be honest," I shrug. "And, it's OK. I mean, he's right."

"About what?"

"The fact that we shouldn't get too comfortable here, none of us. Chatting and getting to know one another is all nice, I mean, after all, we're stuck here and we'll probably be stuck here for a while, but we're in grave danger."

"He's right, and don't get me wrong, I agree with him. When it's a situation like this, a single momentary lack of focus could cost us dearly. But, we can't just walk around one another in this house. We need some social interaction, too, otherwise we'd go crazy," he smiled with those big eyes, not only his lips.

"You know what I'm wondering?" I take up the brown bag and start unpacking it, since he seems to have totally forgotten about the rest of stuff still inside. He joins me, and together, we put everything back in its rightful place.

"What?" he wonders.

"How on earth you two ended up as partners?" I purse my lips, and my eyes widen for just a single moment of wonder.

"Oh, that," he's smiling, but I can tell he didn't expect this question. Perhaps I shouldn't have asked it.

"I'm sorry," I immediately pull back. "I'm prying."

I physically take a step back, feeling my cheeks flushing with a sensation of awkwardness, which now, unfortunately, I can't take back.

"Let's just pretend I didn't ask you this," I add.

"Why?" he gives a half-shrug, as he folds the paper bag evenly over then across, and then places it carefully inside a small kitchen drawer closest to him. "I mean, not like it's something very intimate. Not like you asked me how many girls I slept with," he chuckles, and to my horror, I blush even more.

Did I want to know the answer to that question? No. I don't know. Maybe. But, probably not.

Then, why am I blushing?

"We've been partners for a long time now," he continues, and I'm grateful for not dwelling on the previous comment. "And, where we come from, being partners is much more than just having each other's back."

"What do you mean, where you're from?"

Anderson sighs heavily, then sits at the kitchen table. The soft light of the lamps over his head illuminate his soft freckles and an occasional streak of crow's feet, which become more prominent when he smiles. And yet, it somehow doesn't diminish his charm. It makes it even more prominent. I always believed that old saying of growing old like fine wine was very difficult to achieve, but Anderson is somehow managing it, very successfully.

"Well, I suppose you were bound to find out at some point," he tells me morosely. "I mean, I'm surprised your dad hasn't told you yet, but I guess he has his reasons."

"You keep mentioning my dad," I snap at him, a little more threateningly than I intend to. "But, then you pull back and you just leave me hanging there in the middle."

"Sorry, that's not my intention," he speaks calmly. "I see you here, all a tangled mess, and I just want to help you clarify things, even if it's not my place to do so."

I slump down onto the chair opposite him at the kitchen table. I feel like this conversation would be best conducted sitting down.

"So, can you please tell me what I need to know?" My voice is pleading. Anything is better than not knowing, and whatever he knows about my dad is probably crucial to me.

"Fynn's going to kill me, you know that."

"I'll protect you," I can't help but chuckle. "Now, spill it."

"I guess there is no other way than to do just that," he smiles, with a heavy sigh. "Fynn and I... we belong to an ancient clan of wolf shifters, and - "

"Wait, wait, wait." I lift my hands in a gesture of halt, palms open towards him. "Are you saying you guys can turn into wolves? Like, for real?"

"Yes, that's exactly what I'm saying," he nods, and there isn't a flicker of a smile on his face.

"Well, I'm sorry, but I find it very hard to believe," I snort.

"I'd show you," he starts, "but, despite what movies will have you believe, it's pretty darn painful to do. Our bones actually crack and readjust to make the new form. So, we don't do it just for the heck of it. I believe that I myself have only done it a handful of times. Fynn, too. Only when there is no way out of a situation."

I take a moment to try and let this realization sink in. But, it's difficult. The man in front of me wants me to believe that he can actually turn into a wolf.

"Alright, let's say that I believe you, just for the heck of it," I continue, trying to be calm and composed, but I feel totally opposite from that, "you mentioned that you guys knew my dad from before. You aren't going to tell me that he's a wolf shifter as well, are you?"

"Um, no, not really," he shakes his head and a few strands of his coal black hair fall over his eyes.

"Good," I release a sigh of relief. "Because that I really wouldn't be able to believe."

"We know your dad from way before, when he didn't have all his millions. He was just starting out, and unfortunately, he made a deal with the wrong kind of man. This man was a wolf shifter, and he started to blackmail your father. Your father then came to us, asking for help. We told him that he couldn't give in. Blackmailers, especially like those, would dig their teeth into him and no matter how much money he paid, they would never let him go."

"So, you advised him not to pay?"

"Yes," Anderson nods. "And, even though I still believe we did what we were supposed to do under those circumstances, tragedy followed. It was a tragedy that might have been prevented, but I'm not able to foresee what others will do, so I can't say for certain..."

I realize that he's getting lost in his own thoughts, just talking, as if he doesn't really want to get to the point.

"What tragedy are you talking about?" I urge him.

"It's.... your mother."

The mention of someone who is not to blame for any of this makes my blood boil. I feel my hands clenching into fists in rage, and I want to get up and smash the chair against the floor. Instead, I remain seated, as all the blood rushes to my head.

"What are you saying, Anderson?" I say under my breath.

"Sven was sent to kill your mother because your father wouldn't pay up."

I get up, and bury my face into my hands, as I still keep going around the kitchen. Somehow, I manage to avoid stumbling over anything, or hitting the end of the kitchen table. When I finally reveal my face to Anderson again, I see him looking worried and anxious.

"Are you alright?" he asks, dismayed.

I feel dizzy, like I'm about to lose consciousness. I look to my left and see the kitchen table. My hand reaches out to it, but I miscalculate the distance, and my hand drops down towards the floor, my body following immediately after.

"Maddie!" I hear him shout, but his voice is distant, it sounds like he's stuck in a deep, dark cave, and he's shouting for me to help him out. Or, is it me who's stuck in a cave?

Darkness envelops me, and I can't feel anything anymore. All I hear are the remnants of my mother's voice, fragmented but still warm, caressing my ears, telling me that nothing would be alright ever again.

Chapter 12

F ynn
    I'm sitting on the porch. It's late, but Anderson just returned from the city, so I figured, I'd give him some time to rest. That coffee perked me up enough. I feel like I was thrown on the electric fence and had the good fortune to survive.

Sometimes, these missions weren't that bad. Fresh air, peace and quiet, no one to bug you. That almost makes up for the fact that there's someone out there trying to kill the girl, and us along with her.

I hear the front door open, with a slight cringe. I turn and see Anderson, looking apprehensive.

"Everything alright?" I repeat our current mantra, trying to figure out what's wrong with him.

"I think I messed up, Fynn," he tells me, as he massages the back of his neck with his hand. He's got that I-fucked-up-bad look on his face.

"Fuck," I sigh. "What did you do?"

He doesn't want to say it at first. He just looks at me, as if I have some fortune teller powers, along with my sense of smell. Telepathically, I urge him to spill it. It works.

"I told Maddie about her father."

I frown. "Why would you do a thing like that?"

"She asked," he gives me the stupidest answer, and I feel like punching him in the face right then and there. But, I don't. Like so many other times before. Like the time he thought it would be a good idea to help an old lady cross the street while we were running after a perp. Or, like the time when he thought he'd have another smoke while the drug bust went horribly wrong and half the house was on fire.

Even now, I can't help but think how incredibly lucky this guy is. No matter what he does, things always go his way. I never had that good fortune.

"Don't you think Hugo had a reason not to tell her himself?" I sneer. "And, she asked. The fuck, Anderson. If she asked you to drive her back home, would you do it?"

"Of course not."

"Then, why do this?"

"I felt sorry for her," he tries to explain. "You and I both know what it's like to be kept in the dark about your past."

"This is not about us, Anderson, and you know it."

"I know it, but she deserves to know."

"To know what? That her father is indirectly responsible for her mother's death? Do you even hear yourself?"

I sigh, slumping back into the wicker chair, which has somehow gotten less comfortable in the last minute or so.

"So, now what?" I snort.

"I put her to bed, she felt dizzy when I told her, and almost fell to the floor."

"Great," I roll my eyes. "Just great. We're trying to keep her alive, and you go and almost kill her with a skeleton in her family's closet."

"Don't tell me you think she doesn't deserve to know," he snorts back at me.

"Of course I think she should know, dammit!" I raise my voice. "But, it's not your story to tell. And neither is it mine. You may have destroyed her relationship with the last living member of her family."

"I know..." Anderson looks down, as he always does when he knows he's messed up. But, what's done is done. Feeling sorry won't change anything. "But, I also know that - "

"Shhhh!" I interrupt him, jumping up from my chair.

He knows what that means. His body reacts in the same way. My muscles tighten, my hand pats the handle of my gun. I see him doing the same. He's quiet.

I raise my nose slightly upward. The wind is blowing softly in our direction. The woods are still. I smell sweat, dirty laundry, raunchy mayo.

Silently, I point my finger in the direction of the narrow path that leads from the woods in the distance. We're both on our guard. For a few moments, nothing happens. But, I know it will. My nose is never wrong. My gut is never wrong. And, this time, both are ringing loud and clear.

Anderson is silent. I can barely tell he's by my side. In all these years of being partners, we've adjusted to each other. We know what the other is thinking, and in cases such as this one, it's invaluable. He knows when to be quiet, when to act, when to jump at my mark.

The smell of sweat is getting stronger, the mayo raunchier. I hear the cracking of little branches lost in the fallen leaves, and I know something's coming. My breaths have become shallow, my fingers calm. I've been in this situation more times than I can count. So has Anderson. It could be just a wood critter, but I doubt it. They don't sweat like that. And, then there's the mayo. It's a person, and that's the problem. A person who isn't supposed to be here.

A few more seconds pass by, and someone jumps out of the bushes and into the clearing that opens up into a path. I can't see him well, not as well as I'd like to. The little light on our porch is on. The usual set up is not to make the house look like it's uninhabited. On the contrary, someone should be outside, me or Anderson, and if someone happens to pass by, we should send them on their merry way. Maddie is not to go out or make a peep if there's someone else on the porch or close to it. She has already been instructed on that.

Both Anderson and I wait for the figure to walk closer to us. Whoever it is, he stops every few steps, to take a deep breath. His hands are resting on his back as he does so. It's a he. Now, I'm sure of it. And, I feel even more nervous than a few seconds ago. This isn't a usual trail for hikers. Nor is it the right time of the year. Something just doesn't add up.

The man finally approaches the house, stopping at the foot of the little stairs that lead up to the porch. Anderson and I have both gotten up, and are facing him from the top of the stairs.

"Good evening," the man says, breathing heavily.

He doesn't look in good enough shape for a hiker, especially not for someone who is hiking alone on an unmarked trail.

"Good evening," I reply. Anderson just nods. "Far away from the road, aren't you?"

"I honestly have no idea how I got lost," the man informs us, and the small light on the porch reveals his pale, but reddened, chubby face.

His backpack is small, half empty. The water bottle in the side mesh pocket is half empty as well. His shoes are dirty, dusty, but not worn out. His lightweight jacket is wrapped around his waist, even though it's a chilly night.

"Do you need help?" I ask again.

He looks benevolent. He also looks so out of shape that I think Maddie herself would easily take him on. But, he may be just a clever decoy. It wouldn't be the first time. We put our guard down and it all goes to Hell.

"I think I parked my car somewhere over there," the man points behind our house. "But, I didn't pass your house when I was walking up the path."

"There is no path that leads by our house or even near it," I tell him, my voice not allowing a single ounce of politeness.

I want him gone, but I also want to know what the Hell he's doing here in the first place, because it sure isn't bird watching.

"That's why I'm so confused," the guy continues, sounding lost and helpless.

I know that Anderson would run downstairs, talk to him like they were best friends, show him everything on the map, and maybe even walk him to his car. But, somehow, he doesn't move. I appreciate him going against his first instinct here.

"You got a map?" I ask him again, and he immediately slides the backpack to one side.

My muscles tighten even more, and my hand presses on the bulge in my pants where my gun is. The guy could really be taking out his map only, but he could just as well be taking out a Glock. It's fifty-fifty at this point. But, I'm not revealing anything. My eyes are focused on his backpack, and I know that I'll be able to take him out the moment I see that metallic gleam.

His hand extracts a folded map, one of those really old ones, with scratched and folded edges, and he opens it.

"Now, see this is where I parked," he points at a place on the map, expecting us to know where it is, even though we are not close enough to see it, and neither of us has any intention of getting closer.

"See, that little dirt road down there will take you to another road, and if you just keep going patiently, you'll reach a small exit. That exit will eventually get you to the highway."

"Hmmm," the man seems confused. "That's not the road I came by."

"Well, this is the outback here," I reply quickly. "There are many roads which aren't on the map. It wouldn't surprise me if you took one of those and now you can't find them on the map."

"Is this where we are?" he turns the map to us, and points at something again. "Actually, do you mind if I come up?"

I have to make up my mind quickly. Maddie might make some noise inside. She doesn't know there's someone here. And, if the guy's on the porch, there's no way he wouldn't hear noise from the inside.

"I'll come down, hang on," I quickly make up my mind, invisibly gesturing at Anderson to stay put. "My buddy here and I are watching the house for a friend, and he's a very reclusive kind of guy. No offense."

"Non-taken," the guy replies, as I walk over to him. "I'm Pete, by the way."

"Rod," I tell him. "This here's Hunter."

"Nice to meet you, guys," he says honestly, and it's difficult to believe that he is anything but a lost hiker.

"Same," Anderson nods from the porch.

"Let's see now," I look at the map sprawled open in Pete's hands, and I try to pinpoint our location.

It's hard, because it's mostly greenery on the map where we are. So, I pick a spot at random.

"Here," I tell him, nodding knowingly. "This is exactly where you are."

"How can you tell?" he wonders.

"Our friend's parents bought this house when he was just a kid, and we've all been coming here almost every year since. I know those woods like the back of my hand."

I'm not sure if the guy is buying it, but I'm selling it like our lives depend on it. For all we know, they do.

"Alright then," he nods. "And, I should just go down that road?"

His gaze lifts up at the road that goes around the house and extends somewhere into the darkened distance.

"The road's not on the map," I tell him. "But, trust me. Just go down that road, and you're bound to see a paved road. Take the right turn, and soon enough, you're bound to stumble onto other cars."

"Well," he sighs, "I guess I'll have to take your word for it."

"No other way, buddy," I pat him on the shoulder, a gesture I overtook from Anderson, one I wouldn't be doing of my own accord, but this time, it hit the bull's eye.

Pete's eyes widen in joy, as if I told him a secret, and now we were the best of buddies.

"Must be nice owning a house in the woods, huh?" he looks at the house, and whistles.

I turn to it, and see that Maddie's window is lit up. We need to send this guy packing, before she passes by it and reveals there's someone else here.

"Yeah," I nod. "Or having a friend that does."

"I bet," Pete chuckles, then finally folds his map and puts it back in his backpack. "Thanks for the help, guys."

"No sweat, Pete," I try a smile, and manage one. Anderson just raises his hand in a wave, and we both watch him as he disappears down the road that I pointed him to.

"So, what do you think?" Anderson wonders, when we couldn't see the moving figure any longer.

"I'm not sure," I shake my head. "And, when I'm not sure, then it's not good."

I release a heavy sigh. We'll have to bring in Maddie on this one and tell her about the hiker. I was hoping we wouldn't have to, but this is too much of a coincidence.

We both go inside this time. It'll be a quick watch of a few hours each, as we both need to rest. I let him take the first nap and after getting a quick bite to eat, I get back out on the porch. The sounds of the night are soothing. It's like the whole world wants me to fall asleep. But, I won't. Not now. Especially not now.

Chapter 13

When I walk into the kitchen the following morning, I see Fynn sitting there. He looks troubled, much more than usual.

"Good morning," I call out, a little apprehensively.

I know we sorted everything out, in a way, but it always feels like walking on eggshells around him. I feel like I could say something wrong at any given moment, and he'll be back to his brooding self, snapping at me for no apparent reasons. And, yet, I want to be in the kitchen with him. I want to know why he looks so worried.

"Oh, good morning," he tells me a moment later, when he realizes I'm there.

"You look troubled," I comment. "Much more so than usual, if you don't mind me saying."

"We had a visitor last night," he suddenly tells me, without changing the tone of his voice.

"What?" I almost drop the cup that's in my hands, but instead I put it gently on the kitchen table and sit opposite him. "What visitor?"

"Anderson and I were out, and a hiker walked over to the house. He asked for directions."

He says it in a way that doesn't reveal much about the whole story. So, my gut feeling awakens immediately and starts panicking.

"Was it Sven?"

"Sven?" he repeats, giving me a cross look. "No. We would recognize him. Don't be stupid."

I'm so scared at the potential outcome of this that I don't even pay attention to the comment he just made. I want him to tell me that the guy was just a hiker and nothing else, and that there is absolutely nothing to get worked up about. But, waiting for him, I see he has no intention of doing that.

"So, who was he?"

Fynn just shrugs. His eyebrows are furrowed, brought together all the way close, and the usually fine lines on his forehead have become much more prominent.

"Is he a threat?" I ask again.

"We don't know."

"So, how are you supposed to keep me safe if you have no idea if I'm even in danger right now!?" I snap at him, and my words cut at the air between us like a knife.

He pulls back, and gives me a puzzled look. He isn't angry. But, he should be.

"Are you the cop here?" he growls at me. I don't even grace him with an answer to that obviously rhetorical question. "So, calm down. There is no sign of a threat, at least not at the moment. It's highly unlikely that the guy's a mole, but I wouldn't rule it out either. We just need to stay put, and be twice as vigilant."

"Be sitting ducks, you mean?"

"You wanna try and outrun Sven?" he suddenly pulls his chair back and gets up. "Be my guest. You wouldn't be the first one who tried. But, you'd sure as Hell be the first one who succeeded."

Those words leave me speechless, and I just watch as he walks out of the kitchen, and goes to the living room. I run after him.

"You can't expect me to just - "

The sound of the phone interrupts me, and we both look in the direction where the ringing is coming from. Fynn glances over at me. His eyes are wide, uncertain. He hesitates before he reaches for the phone. In that short amount of time, I managed to take a peek at the screen. It was a hidden number.

"Hello?" Fynn answers after it had been ringing for a while.

I see his face turn pale, as he lowers the phone from his ear and presses a button with a trembling finger. The sound coming from the phone fills up the room.

"Maddie baby?" I hear the voice that makes my blood turn cold. "Do you want to say a few last words to daddy dearest?"

I know that voice. It will always belong to my nightmares, and even in my waking hours, I'll never be able to escape it.

"Maddie?" my dad speaks, his voice trembling. He coughs a little.

"You need to excuse daddy dearest, he doesn't feel very well. And, I'm afraid he won't be feeling much better than this ever again," Sven chuckles violently.

Fynn isn't saying anything. I look at him for help, but all he is doing is holding that damn phone.

"Dad?" I manage to muster, on the verge of tears.

"Sweetheart, it's fine... don't worry..." my dad sounds tired, his words are garbled, like he's got something in his mouth.

"Dad... I..." The realization of what he did is on the tip of my tongue, but I can't say it. "I love you..."

"I love you, t - "

"Oh, isn't that sweet," Sven drags his snake-like voice. "But, I didn't call for that. Fynn, you there?"

"Yeah, I'm here, you piece of shit," Fynn growls, as his jaw tightens under the strain.

"Good to hear your voice," Sven hisses. "It'll be even better to kick your ass, but I'll leave that for up close and personal."

"How did you get this number?" Fynn speaks through clenched teeth, rage oozing out of his words.

"A magician never reveals his secrets," Sven chuckles. "Haven't you learned that already?"

"I swear, when I lay my hands on you - "

"You'll probably be left without them," Sven interrupts him. "Now, Maddie baby, say goodbye to daddy. He has to go away for a very long time."

"No!" I scream at the phone, bending my whole body over it, my hands pleading at the voice that materializes out of that little gadget. "Dad! If you touch - "

At that moment, a single gunshot explodes somewhere inside the phone, and the connection breaks.

"Dad!" I scream again, dropping down to my knees.

I'm barely aware of the hands that are around me, but I recognize the smell. Fynn lets me sob on his shoulder, his big palms resting on my back and the nape of my neck. I'm shaking. I feel like someone had pulled the carpet right from underneath me, like I'm standing at the edge of a cliff, and someone just pushed me. Now, I'm falling, just falling, and I have no idea where it will end, or how hurtful it will be when I finally hit the ground.

My body is trembling still. I've stopped sobbing. I've stopped repeating the word dad over and over again. My tears keep streaming down my face, an endless waterfall of sadness with no end in sight.

Fynn doesn't say anything. He just lets me be me, my sad self, as we both try to accommodate to the shock we just survived. I just can't forget the sound of that gunshot. Was it aimed at my dad? And, if it was, did it hit him? If it did hit him, is he alright? Has he survived? Will I ever see him again?

So many questions are swarming inside my mind, each of them stinging me like an angry bee. It takes all my effort to finally calm down a little. I lift my gaze to meet Fynn's. He is as grave as ever. I know I could never ask him to console me. Would he even know what to say? But, he is here, not Anderson. And, I need him.

"Do you think my dad's alright?" I whisper, feeling the salty taste of my tears in the corner of my mouth.

He sighs heavily before replying. He lets go of me, and we both get up from the floor.

"I doubt it, Maddie," he tells me the truth.

A part of me appreciates his honesty. That's what I need right now. I can't get lost in daydreams that will end up killing me. But, another part of me wants to squeeze my fists and start hitting him with all my might, because how dare he assume that my father is dead. My mind is screaming with pain, my heart can't stop skipping every other beat, and I feel like I can barely stand up.

"I think I need to lie down a little," I feel like I'm reliving the same scene from before, only it's much more difficult this time.

A sudden sensation of nausea hits me like a tidal wave. I bend over and throw up the remnants of my sandwich and coffee. It feels like it lasts forever, getting all of it back out, and when I'm finally done, my stomach contracts a few more times, but nothing more comes out. The stench hits me like a ton of bricks, as I wipe the corner of my mouth with my upper hand.

"I'm... sorry..." I manage to say weakly.

"Don't worry about it," he is quick to reply. "I'll clean that up. Let's get you to bed now."

Unsteady and weak, I allow him to take me to my room. I feel the cold, wet cloth as he wipes my face. Sleep takes over me violently, like a tornado, promising no rest. Only more turmoil.

Chapter 14

Anderson
I doubt I'd been asleep for longer than an hour or so, and yet it seems like I missed everything. Fynn quickly updated me on what happened over the phone, and I see he's out of his mind. Even though, just by looking at him, you'd never tell. He is that good at hiding it. But, I see his fingers. They're not calm, as usual. They're the only part of his body that always betrays him when he's like this.

"So, that's why I think we should head over there now," Fynn wraps up telling me exactly what happened, and suggesting to go and hide somewhere else, somewhere where not even the police would know where we are.

"Is it still safe?" I wonder. "We haven't been there in about..."

"Five years," he reminds me. "Luckily, we didn't need to use it. The police safe houses, any of the ones we used, did the job. But, this time, we're screwed."

"You think the hiker had something to do with the call?"

"Everything points to the contrary, but it can't be a coincidence. It just can't."

"You know I trust you when it comes to smells and gut feelings," I remind him.

"I know," he tries a smile. "Thanks. Really."

"So, we wake her up and get going?"

"I think so," he nods, drumming his fingers silently against the kitchen table, as if following an inside rhythm which is trying to soothe him, only not very successfully. "Just get what we need the most. Some food. Water. Leave the rest. We need to go now."

"OK."

"Actually, you go get the girl," he tells me. "I'll grab stuff from the kitchen. Just shove her stuff in her bag and don't spend too much time on it. I'll be waiting outside by the car."

"Sure thing," I nod again, and rush over to Maddie's room.

I wasn't in on the conversation, but judging from what Fynn told me, Sven either knows where we are or he'll know very soon. And then, there'll be Hell to pay. We need to get the heck out of here and now.

With those thoughts in mind, I knock on Maddie's door, and immediately enter without even waiting for the OK. She's lying on the bed, her entire body covered with a blanket. She's breathing slowly, evenly. She's fully asleep and I almost feel bad for waking her up. But, there's no time to spare.

"Maddie," I call out to her, shaking her gently on the shoulder.

She stirs a little underneath the blanket, but doesn't acknowledge me.

"Maddie, you need to wake up," I tell her again, a little more loudly. "We need to go."

She stirs some more, her eyes barely open, a faint flicker of recognition. Then, she props herself up on her elbows, as her chestnut hair falls in thick tresses behind her on the pillow.

"Go where?" she asks, fully awakened now by the newfound knowledge.

"Can't tell you," I shake my head, as I pull the blanket off of her. "It's Fynn's place. Well, not technically. He doesn't live there. But, he's used it for years. It's abandoned, and perfect for what we need." I realize I'm babbling, but that's me on edge. Fynn's fidgety. I yack like a bored old grandma with her nose in everybody's business.

"Oh..." she nods, rubbing her eyes. "Well, lemme just get ready and
- "

"No time," I shake my head, already up from the bed and grabbing the few items of clothes she's brought with her from the shelves. "Where's your bag?"

She points at a little backpack in the corner, and I shove all her stuff in there. I grab her toothbrush and toothpaste from the bathroom and two towels.

"You ready to go?" I ask her.

Her eyes are sparkling in the darkness. I can't tell if she's trying to suppress the tears. I squeeze her shoulder.

"Hey…" I tell her. "I know it looks bad, but you have no proof that your dad took that shot."

She lifts her diamond eyes to me, and I see hope in them, hope unlike any other I've seen in all my years on the force.

"But, Fynn said - "

"I thought I told you to take into account that Fynn's an asshole sometimes," I remind her, and the joke works. She bursts into laughter, and two large glistening tears roll down her cheeks. "He thinks he's got the Universe by the balls or something, and I love that guy to death, but sometimes, he's got his head so deep up his ass that he has no idea what he's saying."

She chuckles again.

"So, let's focus on us first, and getting out of this house safe and sound. Then, once all this is over, I promise you that we'll find out what happened to Hugo. Let's not jump to conclusions before we got all the facts straight. Alright?"

She takes us both by surprise when she jumps at me and wraps her arms around my neck. For a moment, I don't know what to do, and just stand there stupidly, with her hanging from my neck, all elongated and swan-like. But then, instinct takes over, and I envelop her into a warm hug. She fits into my arms so perfectly, like she was made to be there.

She looks up at me, her cheeks still red and her eyes a little swollen, but she's still the most beautiful girl I've ever laid my eyes on. No matter how many times I repeat to myself that this is a case we're working on, a very delicate one at that, I can't pretend like there isn't chemistry between us.

It's hard not to lower my head just a few inches towards her and press my lips against hers. I can't. I want to, with all my heart, but I know I can't. I keep staring at her, so sweet, so vulnerable, so willing. Her lips part slightly, and her warm breath spills onto me. I dig my fingers deeper into her flesh. I press her closer to me. I can feel her heart beat against mine, beating in unison.

Finally, I let go of her. I know I can't do this. I'm not allowed. I'm the older one here, and should know better.

"Everything's going to be fine," I resort to the usual phrase that is said under these circumstances, and it provides some distance from the overly intimate moment we just shared.

She nods. I feel sorry that the magic is broken, but it's better that way.

"Come on, I got your stuff here," I pat the backpack in my arms. "We need to get going now."

"Let's go," she says, still weak, but willing to obey.

We walk out of the house, and I grab a few other things on the way. Outside, Fynn is standing by the car, cigarette in his mouth. When he sees us, he inhales deeply, then drops the rest of it to the ground and stomps on it angrily. I don't have to be near him to know that all the hairs on his body are pricked up. He is trying to pick up a sense of a possible intruder, but he isn't agitated. He is focused, calm.

"You ready?" he asks quickly. I can barely hear him.

A few leaves ruffle in the bushes close to us. All three pairs of eyes focus on it.

"Just a hedgehog," Fynn assures us.

Maddie is scared stiff. I help her to the car. She gets in the back. I throw the backpack into the trunk, then sit shotgun. I'll let Fynn drive this time, and maybe even catch some shuteye. Seems like nothing's going according to plan. These scenarios are already nerve-wracking enough, even when it all does go according to plan. But, this... I dare not think what awaits us by the end.

Chapter 15

We drive for what seems to be a small eternity, and I keep dozing on and off in the car. My anxiety and fear are keeping me awake, but the softly fluctuant ride on the occasional bumpy road lulls me to sleep. I think of my mother's loving smile. I remember my father's strong arms and how they always made me feel so safe. Now, I wonder if there is any place in the world which I could call that. I doubt it.

And yet, one glance forward is enough for me to calm down, at least a little. I see Fynn's eyes in the rear view mirror. I see the determination in them. I see a promise. I can't see Anderson. All I get are the random pops of his curls that appear from behind his seat. I don't see it, but I know he turns around from time to time, to check up on me. My eyes are closed, but it's one of those looks you can feel, even when enshrouded in darkness.

We arrive in the early hours of the morning. Fynn gets out of the car first, then Anderson. He opens the door for me, and when I exit, I realize we're in the middle of nowhere again.

"This is an even bigger middle of nowhere than last time," I say, feeling an unexpected surge of optimism. I attribute it to the rising sun in the distance and the sweet chirping of the birds from a nearby tree. The bushes are thick, hiding the view from us.

"That's exactly what we're looking for," Anderson nods. "Fynn, lead the way. It's been ages since you brought me here, I doubt I'd find the way in myself."

"Just follow the road," Fynn tells us.

"What road?" Anderson wonders.

Instead of reply, Fynn points his index finger. It takes a while to find a small clearing in the bushes, and once we push some of the branches aside, we see a slightly trodden path.

"You can only find it if you know what you're looking for," Fynn explains, leading the way.

"Good old Fynn," Anderson smiles, going last, urging me to go before him.

The road is narrow, there are branches scratching us from all sides, but we keep going. Finally, we see a door, behind a padlocked gate. My first thought is that someone had closed up Fynn's place, and we wouldn't be able to get in. But, then, Fynn's hand dives into his pocket and extracts the key which opens up the lock in seconds. The door screeches as it moves, slowly and unforgivingly, but finally, the door itself opens as well. A damp smell of mildew hits my nostrils. I cough a little.

"I'm afraid it doesn't smell like the Ritz," Anderson chuckles. "Even I can smell that."

I turn to him, not getting the joke.

"Oh, you don't know," Anderson slaps his forehead jokingly. "Of course you don't. I had this treehouse when I was a kid. My dad built it for me. My mom added the little touches, you know, like the curtains. I mean, I hated those things. I thought the guys would all make fun of me for that. I got this awesome treehouse and the windows have curtains. Like, what the fuck, right?" He pauses as he tells me the story, and I can actually feel the warmth of his memory. "But, eventually, I grew to love those horrid flowery things. It just made the place more of a home away from home. Even though the home was right there. I could see the house from the treehouse, but I was still far enough away to consider it my own little castle."

"Boy, when you tell a story, you really take it from the top, don't you?" Fynn snorts.

"You're just complaining because you heard it before," Anderson replies, then continues. "So, as I was saying, my friends and I were at the treehouse one day, being boys. You know, smoking, maybe looking at porn magazines I stole from my dad, maybe not, I'm not saying this one for sure." I laugh, as Fynn disappears through the door.

I hesitate to follow. I turn to Anderson.

"Let's finish the story outside, and then we'll go in, how's that?" he seems to sense my apprehension, and I feel a wave of gratitude. "So, we're smoking and suddenly, one of my friends drops his cigarette, and the whole place catches fire like that. We're all sliding down the ladder, waiting for one another. I, as the proud and now infamous owner of the treehouse am left last. I wanted to make sure everyone got out safely before I rush down myself. But, by the time everyone was out, the fire was raging, and it caught my pants. I managed to put it out, and finally rushed down the ladder, following the others, but I inhaled too much smoke. I spent two weeks at the hospital after that, I could barely talk during those two weeks. That's when they told me that I'm left with about 15% of my sense of smell. But, I should consider myself lucky, I guess. We could have burned to death, all of us. It's weird how it all happens so quickly, like flicking a light switch. On. Off. And poof. You're no more."

"But, you should be really proud of yourself, too," I remind him. "You made sure everyone got out before you did. That's something."

"Now that I consider it, I guess so. But, back then, I wasn't thinking about it. It was just the right thing to do and I just did it. As simple as that."

He shrugs as he speaks, and I see a glimmer of the boy he once was. Short shorts, skinned knees, dirt underneath his fingernails. That's how I imagine him. Fynn - not so much. He sounds like the kid who'd shoosh you in the library for whispering too loudly.

"You guys coming, or what?" Fynn appears at the door, as if called upon.

Anderson and I smile at each other, and I enter first. Still in a good mood from the story I just heard, I don't mind the smell of mildew so much any longer. I realize it's an entrance to a mine, and they made it into a big, elongated hallway. It probably gets pretty cold in here in the winter months, so hopefully we won't stay here long enough to find out exactly how cold it gets.

"These things over here are mine," Fynn points at several black bags filled to the brim and closed up in the corner, so it's impossible to guess what's inside, based on the shape of the bag alone.

"In other words, we won't be getting near those," Anderson adds.

I appreciate his light jokes. They allow me to escape the grim reality of my current existence, if only for a short while.

"There are two beds over there," Fynn points. "You can choose which one you'd like," he tells me. "Anderson and I will use the other one. We'll never be asleep at the same time anyway, so not like everyone needs their own bed."

"Good point," I nod.

I can see that Fynn is still on edge, much more than Anderson and I are. Or, maybe, we're just better at hiding it.

"So, we're safe here?" I wonder aloud, and both guys turn to look at me.

"I doubt there's anywhere we're a hundred percent safe, but this is the next best thing," Fynn assures us both, and I get the feeling, he's trying to convince himself equally of this. "We'll stay here for as long as we need to."

"Are we letting the boss know?" Anderson asked.

"We'll tell him we moved," Fynn explains. "And, we'll tell him we're safe. But, we won't tell him where we are."

"Won't he be pissed?" Anderson watches him, head askew.

"Pissed or not, that's how things are going down," Fynn sounds like that is the end of the conversation for him. "I think I need some shuteye, so you'll take the first shift."

"Sure thing," I see Anderson nod, without a single word or gesture of disobedience.

"You mind if we take this one?" Fynn asks me, pointing at one of the beds, which in no way differed from the other one, apart from its slightly different location.

"No, I'm fine with whichever," I assure him, secretly glad that, at least, he was nice enough to ask.

"Alright then," he concludes, walking over to the bed, quickly kicking off his shoes, and then just slumping down with the entire weight of his body onto it.

Anderson shrugs his shoulders with a helpless look on his face, but I know now that there's so much more underneath it. Their relationship is one that seems to transcend mere partnership in the traditional sense of the word, and I believe it has much to do with where they came from. Their roots are the same, so much different from mine. I want to understand them more, despite the fact that everything is telling me I can't get close to them.

I watch as Anderson leaves outside, for his watch. I count his footsteps. I listen to Fynn's soft breathing. Somehow, against all odds, I feel safe.

Chapter 16

"There's no reception here of any sort, is there?" I sigh looking at the thick, high walls around us.

"Not like you'd need it, anyway," Anderson tells me.

It's been a few days of our stay here, without a big choice of books or any other entertainment, apart from talking. Fynn has offered me one of those mystery bags he has in the corner, the one that contains books, a chessboard and some cards. I suppose, only books serve my purpose. The other two would require the active presence of another person, or maybe even two of them. Fynn has made it perfectly clear that getting too close would be wrong. It'd be too dangerous for us all. And, I know what he means. I know exactly what he means. But, despite that, I can't order my heart what to feel.

"Yeah, not like I have my phone on me," I snort.

"Are you bored with us already?" he chuckles.

I lift my head, and I just can't remain serious. I wonder what he's like when there isn't death in the air around him. Is he equally fun and amusing, or maybe even more so? What is he like when he's in love?

I bite my lip at the thought, as he turns his back to me, and rummages through one of Fynn's bags.

"You shouldn't do that," I tell him, glancing at the door.

Fynn is still out, keeping an eye out on the area.

"Oh, trust me, there's nothing I haven't done to him, that he hasn't forgiven me," Anderson grins, then dives even more deeply into the bag.

"I can't imagine him forgiving anything," I say, even though I meant to keep this to myself.

"You, and many others," he nods, finally extracting something out of the bag.

Judging from the look on his face, it was exactly what he was looking for.

"You'd better put that back."

"No way," he shakes his head.

I still can't see the thing in his hand properly, as he looks at it tenderly, almost lovingly.

"We'll make this baby work," I hear him say, extending his hands to me, and I see it's one of those old radios. "This baby right here is a Pioneer SX-850 series, a typical AM/FM stereo receiver from the 1970's."

"The '70s?" I repeat.

"It has an outstanding FM reception, we just need to see if there is a good external antenna."

He put the radio down on a small table in the corner, and went to rummage some more in that same bag.

"Got it!" he shouted victoriously, holding an antenna in his hand.

"Will it work?" I ask.

"Will it work?" he repeats, accentuating every word. "It sure as Hell will work."

He looks around, still looking for something.

"Ah!" he shouts, rushing over to his backpack and getting out a screwdriver. "Now, we're talking!"

He sits down on the floor, and gets to work. I watch as his fingers dance around the little machine which seems all but broken. It gets twisted, opened, the closed once more. The wires that are poking out are all tucked nicely in. The antenna is first resting wobbly, but he fixes that, too. When he is finished, he gets up, actually jumps up from the floor, and places the radio on the little table.

"There," he tells me.

"You made it work?" I ask.

"Let's see if I did," he replies, proudly.

The look on his face tells me how much he enjoys doing these kinds of things. He gets the wire from the back and attaches it to a power source. His fingers find the button dial easily, turning it slowly. He looks like he knows exactly what he's doing. At first, there is no sound. A few seconds pass, and I don't have the heart to tell him the obvious. But, he keeps on twisting and turning, and I just wait for him to give up on his own.

Some more time passes, but he's still immersed into it. I place my hand on his shoulder, but he pays no attention to it. He is too focused on the little radio. His lips purse in invisible effort, his eyebrows furrow.

Suddenly, we hear a crackle, soft, but it's discernible.

"Ha!" he shouts victoriously once again. "What did I tell you?"

I smile at his fervor, and let him go on. The more he is twisting the dial, the more noise arises out of that little thing, as if it is doing its best to do what we expect of it. The first, inaudible words reach us, and the triumphant look on his face is even more prominent. Slowly, the words are substituted by melody. He manages to clear up the reception, and the room around us is filled with the sound of music.

"I can't believe you did that!" I shout, enjoying the song, swaying my hips to the side.

"So, should I take it that you didn't have faith in me?" he asks, teasingly. "For shame, Maddie. For. Shame."

We both burst out into loud laughter at the same time.

"Come on," he suddenly offers me his hand.

For a moment, I'm not sure what he wants me to do, but it becomes crystal clear. He wants us to dance. It's no waltz or anything similar, where an old fashioned couple needs to follow a certain set of rules, luckily. It's just a song. No big deal. Not like accepting this dance means I'm promising myself to him. So, I accept.

The moment I put my hand into his, he kicks his left leg forward, and swirls me with sharp precision. I can't suppress a giggle. So, I don't. My calf muscles flex, as the entirety of my being advances towards him, following the rhythm around us. His hands are holding mine. There is a certain control about it, his poised strike and movement are demanding, and yet giving at the same time.

I've never been a good follower of the rhythm, but with him, it's easy. I'm just following the sequences of his body, realizing how much I've needed this, how much I needed his hands in mine, his presence so close to me. The feelings are almost crippling. But, instead of taking power away from me, it bestows more power onto me, and I can't stop laughing, as he swirls me around the room, and all I see are his sparkling eyes.

We advance, move forward, and then move back. We pirouette, his arms around my waist, then both our arms high up above our heads. There are no rules. Just pure enjoyment. Our heads are swaying, I feel like I'm unburdened by my clothes, I feel as light as air.

Suddenly, the music stops, and we end up facing each other, so close that I can feel the warmth of his breath on the tips of my lips. His touch is electrifying. I feel like I'm standing a few inches up from the ground, almost floating, and it's all because of him.

My lips are dry. I feel like I haven't had a drink of water in days. I swallow heavily. His eyes are staring deeply into mine, relentless, not letting go. I'm not even sure I want him to let go. My mind has no idea what is right, and what is wrong. All I know is that his presence feels so good. It can only be right, no?

He leans a little closer to me, our lips almost touching. Our bodies follow suit. I'm trembling.

Just as he's about to press his lips against mine, we hear the front door open.

"Anderson, are you - "

Fynn sees us standing like that, too close for comfort. I know what's going through his mind. I know, because the same thoughts have been swarming my mind for days now, ever since this whole nightmare started. Only, I can't even say that it's a nightmare, because I met these two men.

"What's going on here?" he asks, sternly, as if we are two students caught making out by the bleachers, and he's the teacher responsible for keeping order among the students.

"Nothing," Anderson replies first, taking a step back, and letting go of me.

"Doesn't look like nothing," Fynn snorts.

I feel his cold stare all the way down to my heels. I never thought someone's icy stare would get to me this much. I want to start explaining everything that led to this awkward moment. I want to tell him that we didn't expect any of this to happen. We were just dancing, nothing else. But, I can't move. I can't say a word. All I can do is feel guilty underneath his stare.

"We were just dancing, that's all," Anderson keeps on explaining, even though we all know full well what was about to happen.

It doesn't take a rocket scientist to know.

I almost feel like chuckling to myself, because this seems exactly like the kind of thing Anderson would say to lighten up the mood. But, I'm not laughing. I'm not even smiling. I feel like I'm torn between these two men, a constant fight between hot and cold, fire and ice, and I'm not sure how much more of this I can take.

"A little too close then."

"Well, you know, we got into the rhythm," Anderson, being his usual joker self, has to try.

But, Fynn isn't letting it go. His stare is still chilling me to my very bones, transferring a message. Why? Why, when I warned you once already?

I feel like I've somehow disappointed him, even though I didn't do anything. Nothing happened. But, I can't say that nothing was going to happen. That would be a lie. I still remember the heat of Anderson's presence. I remember his gaze. He could light me up with just the touch of his hands. I wonder what would happen to me if we actually kissed. Would I go all weak in the knees? Would I melt like honey in his hands? Those all sound about right.

Not wanting to reveal any of this, I remain quiet, letting Anderson handle this delicate situation, even though he is also not doing it all that well. Feeling guilty, I just watch him squirm, not being able to offer much help.

"A word, outside?" Fynn growls at Anderson, and I feel a strange relief hoping I'm off the hook.

However, this isn't all Anderson's fault. I could have refused his hand. I could have refused the dance. I didn't. And, there isn't a parallel universe in existence where I did.

Chapter 17

F^{ynn}

"What the fuck do you think you're doing!?" I snarl at Anderson, the moment we're outside.

The nature around us is in stark contrast to my mood right now, and I couldn't care less about the freakin' birds singing or the sun shining above us. All I want is to knock some sense into Anderson, since he obviously hasn't got much left in him, to do what he was trying to do just now.

"Unwinding," Anderson replies, scoffing at me. "You should try it sometimes. It won't kill you."

"Are you serious!?" I try to keep my voice down, but it's damn near impossible. "You call that unwinding? After all the talking we had on the subject?"

"What talking?" he shrugs, staying irritatingly calm. I always hate him for that. "You talked. You always talk. I'm usually silent, and you don't even check to see whether I agree or not."

"I'm trying to keep us safe. What's so wrong with that?"

I turn around and kick a wandering stone that happens to cross my path. It flies off somewhere into the bushes. No sound follows it. There are no woodland critters around here, and the thought calms me down a little. At least that. It's just us.

"The problem is that we can't be safe, if we're going after what we need," he explains, and I know exactly what he's referring to. "Don't tell me it didn't occur to you," I suddenly hear him say, and as if following the same instinct, we glance at the door. It's still closed.

She won't be coming outside. She doesn't want to be a part of this conversation. And, she'd better stay inside. I can't shout at her like I can shout at Anderson, whom I've known for years.

I snort loudly. He doesn't wait for me to say anything to that.

"Because I have," he adds quickly.

"You think that's not obvious?" I shake my head at him disapprovingly.

What the fuck is he thinking – fucking with someone we're supposed to protect and keep safe? I'm so pissed I can't think straight. I see red everywhere.

"No, what's strange is that it isn't obvious to you," he shakes his head at me. "Have you seen her? Have you spoken to her?"

I don't like the direction where this is going. I know what he's going to say now. He's going to say she's perfect for us. She's perfect for what we need. In a way, he's right. He's totally fucking right, but there is no way we can act on that. How the fuck does he not see that?

"What difference does that make?" I shout, lost in my own angry thoughts.

"There you go again," Anderson clenches his jaw at me. "Your brain is wracking itself, never stopping, always on guard, but you don't even see what it is you're missing."

"I see what I'm missing," I sneer.

"Do you?" Anderson stares me down. We remain like that for a few moments, neither of us willing to look away first. So, neither of us does. "Do you really?"

"Your problem is that you think anyone is a good fit," I speak, and I feel the heat in my tingling skin.

I know for a fact that this isn't true. Finding a mate is damn right hard. We haven't been able to find anyone in ages, and I think that we've both almost given up hope. Only neither of us has expressed that hopelessness yet.

"I told her about us," his revelation hits me like a ton of bricks.

"You what!?"

"I did," he shrugs, as if it was totally out of his hands, and all he could do was just sit there and watch. "You should have seen her. She accepted it. She accepted us. She never questioned it."

"That means nothing," I snort, shaking my head at him, at myself, at the possibility that has just opened itself for us.

"That means a lot, Fynn, and you know it." Anderson's head jerks backward. "If we don't find someone, our clan will die out."

"You don't fucking need to remind me of that. Because, that's exactly why we need to be careful."

I feel that ancient calling of our ancestors deep in my bones. I know Anderson feels it, too. Like the calling of some long forgotten animal, or one that is in danger of becoming extinct. I guess, that's exactly what we'll become, if we don't do something about it. And, soon.

"I know we can't throw caution to the wind," he's talking more calmly now. I know he doesn't want to argue, and neither do I. "But, we can't wait any longer either. Fate just drops this girl into our lap, and she's perfect. Fynn, she's fucking perfect. Have you taken a good look at her? Jeez!"

I don't even need to dignify that with a reply. Of course I took a fucking look at her. That's all I've been doing since this whole thing started.

"I know it's been hard since..."

"Don't talk about her," I growl. "This has nothing to do with her."

"It does, and it doesn't," Anderson approaches me and places his hand on my shoulder. "I know. You don't have to tell me anything. I've known you my whole life, and I can see through that mask you put on. You believe it was your fault."

"It was my fault."

We haven't really talked much about this, even though he started a few times. But, this is something that is mine to deal with. Mine, and no one else's.

"No, it was a tragic set of circumstances," Anderson continues, even though I'm not buying a word of what he's selling. "We lost her, but it's not your fault."

"How many goddamn times are you gonna repeat that?" I scoff at him.

"As many times as it's necessary for you to believe it," he growls back at me. "You usually don't listen to me, but do so now. Maddie is... she's the fucking answer to our prayers. You just need to make sure you don't scare her away."

I sigh, turning around, wetting my lips with my tongue. I could really use a drink right now. And, maybe a wall to punch really hard. That'd help calm me down. But, instead I just cross my arms across my upper abdomen.

"We'll sort this shit out," he assures me. "We always do, don't we?"

"You're way too optimistic, you know that."

"And, that saved our asses more than once, didn't it?" he grins, and I have to admit he's right. We make a good team, partly because of our stark contrast personalities.

Anderson can still see a diamond in a damn pigsty, while I see shit even among the cleanest diamonds. Ying and fucking yang.

"Shit, Anderson," I rake my fingers through my hair, "I wouldn't even know where to begin."

"From the beginning is always good."

We both chuckle at this, even though I'm still not buying it. It's too messy. There's too much stuff that is preventing this from happening.

"We need to finish this first," I tell him. "We can't fuck up."

"My thoughts exactly."

"We can't let her down," I shake my head. "We need to do what we promised we would, and then, we can ask her..."

"There you go with the asking again," Anderson is rolling in the aisles again. "That's not how this works. You don't just ask a girl, oh hey, you're pretty good-looking and kinda sweet, how's about you be the mother to our wolf shifter children?"

I'm listening to him laugh, and of course, when he puts it like that, it always sounds so ridiculous. I guess I'm just too old-fashioned sometimes. For fuck's sake, I can't even remember the last time I kissed a girl, let alone something else.

"You need to charm her, make her fall for you," he explains.

"Sure, easy for you to do," I snort.

Standing by his side, he makes me look like Victor Frankenstein's hunchback assistant. Anderson's got it all - looks and charm. Me - neither. If you like me, you like me for some really messed up reason probably you yourself aren't even fully aware of. The thought makes me smile, however.

"So, you've calmed down a little?" he asks me.

"Mhm," I nod. "It's all good. But, we're still not doing anything. And by we, I mean you."

"Cross my heart," he uses his index finger to actually make a cross over his heart. "You talked to the Chief?"

"Yeah," I nod again. "Explained what happened. Didn't tell him where we were though."

"Did he ask?"

"Several times," I nod. "But, I think we got a mole. No way they could have found us back there, unless someone at the station ratted us out."

"That's possible."

"So, now we do it our way. The Chief can kiss my ass if he doesn't like it, I don't care. He can suspend me later on, if he wants to. But, I'm bringing this girl home safe and sound."

"That's the Fynn I know and love," Anderson smiles, patting me on the shoulder.

"So, he eventually agreed to my plan, and just said to keep a low profile wherever we are."

"The phone?"

"Used a burner," I explain. "And, I got rid of it. I should be heading into town tomorrow, for some supplies, and to get another one."

"Want me to go?" he offers.

"No," I shake my head. "Stay with Maddie. She needs you. You can console her much better than I ever could."

"That's only because you never really tried."

His words make me think. Feelings are not my strong suit. They never have been. I rely on my brains, never on a gut feeling or whatever you wanna call it. And, girls are all feelings. Maddie obviously more so than others. No wonder she prefers Anderson's presence to mine.

Not that it matters that much. I don't question who I am, or how I act. I just am. You can't change the nature of who you are. You can't even soften it that much. If someone accepts you as you are, great. If not – well, then it was never meant to be.

I'm much too practical to dwell on such notions. I'll just go do what needs to be done, and he can stay behind and be a shoulder to cry on. That's what you call proper division of labor.

"But, you better keep your hands where I can see them. And, don't let your guard down, even for a second," I remind him.

We both remember Sven. It doesn't take us much more than a few moments to remind ourselves of the carnage that animal leaves behind him. You never know what to expect of him. He sounds all nice and polite, then you turn your back to him and he'll stab you before you can blink.

"Alright then," Anderson breaks the silence first. "I'll go back inside. Unless you want me to take over?"

"No," I shake my head. "Go see how she's doing. She's probably confused by what just happened and how I reacted. Try to explain the situation again, just don't mention anything about what we talked about. That's a conversation for a whole other time."

"Sure."

His reply is brief, and he quickly disappears from my sight. I take a deep breath, wondering why I reacted like that in the first place. Slowly, a long forgotten green-face with deep, elongated claws shows itself. I didn't even know it still existed inside of me. And yet, here is it. Brought to the surface.

"You like her..." the voice speaks into my ear.

The voice is my own, and yet, it's not. It is the voice of my wise self, the voice that has been silent for such a long time, simply because there was nothing it could say. Now, I hear it, and it feels like a new dawn.

Chapter 18

A few days pass by without much happening. I suppose that is a good thing. Sometimes, we all talk about irrelevant things. Other times, we are all lost in our own individual thoughts, thinking about all those things that used to make us happy back when we were actually living our lives, and not hiding away. But, necessity makes victims of us all sometimes. And, I can't complain. They have been taking such good care of me. Fynn brought us some snacks and special foods we told him, so it's all about the little things nowadays.

But, at the same time, there is just too much pressing down onto me, and I feel like it is getting harder and harder to breathe. This place is safe, but it is slowly becoming claustrophobic. I've never suffered from any such ailment, but even the strongest minds can succumb to such pressures.

One afternoon, I notice that Anderson is sleeping soundly on the bed opposite mine. He looks so peaceful. Covered with a thin blanket, he is facing the opposite wall. His breathing is rhythmical and steady. I wonder if he is dreaming. I am. Every single night. And, it's always one of the two extremes. I'm either buried in some coffin, and Sven is shoveling dirt on top of me, screaming that no one will ever find me again, or I'm back home with my dad, in his study, and we are leafing through the family album, with this whole nightmare completely behind us.

I wonder if that moment would ever come. I wonder if I would ever see him again. But, I need to stay positive. I can't let depression sink its teeth into me. I just can't.

So, I tiptoe outside, and run into Fynn, who is on guard duty.

"Nice day," I say, as he gazes at something in the distance.

A few birds are chirping somewhere far away, and they catch my attention. I see there is a small path around our hideout, maybe even a nearby woods. I wonder if I'd be allowed to take a walk, as the place has become suffocating, despite the fact that I know both of them are trying to make it pleasant for me.

"Rain's coming," he tells me.

Only then do I realize that he is looking into the horizon. The sky over us is blue, so light blue that you wish to dive right into it, without even looking. But, the horizon reveals something more menacing. Dark grey clouds are clustering together, and that is never a good sign. Still, they seem far away, probably a whole day away.

"That might not be so bad," I smile. "It'll freshen up the air a little."

He doesn't say anything to that, and I guess I don't expect him to. Expecting things from Fynn is close to madness, mostly because he never reacts the way you expect him to. He doesn't have normal people reactions. His are always over the top. You just try to steer clear of it, even though that is the last thing I want to do. I want to get to know him, but I have no idea how. He's not the least bit interested in small talk, and that is basically the only thing we can do around here. How does one approach him? How does one show him it's OK to let your guard down and just relax for a while?

"Listen, I wanted to ask you something..." I start, twirling a loose strand of hair around my index finger, something I always did with my dad. The action used to bring me back to the past, to my childhood years, when I would mostly get everything I wished for. All I had to do was point at it and it would be mine.

He turns to me, his eyes piercing, but at the same time looking through me and all around me. It's like he is trying to frame me into the surroundings, so he gives me all the attention I need, not once neglecting to notice what is going on around us.

"I noticed there is a small path around here," I continue, slightly hesitant, pointing somewhere behind him. It doesn't seem like something he'd agree to, but one needs to ask if one is to be given, right?

"And, I was wondering if I could maybe go take a quick walk? You know, just to clear my head a little and - "

"No," he cuts me like a knife. "It's too dangerous."

"I know that, but..." I start, but I'm not really sure where I'm going with this one, as all I have are my wishes, and not proper arguments.

My father always said that in order to convince someone of something, you need to make them see it from your point of view. Then, they would usually agree to go along with whatever it is you are asking of them. However, if all you had were feelings, then achieving this was slightly more complicated. Still, if you have solid arguments which make sense, then you've got it made. Unfortunately, this wasn't one of those cases.

"It's too dangerous to separate, and especially for you to go anywhere on your own."

My gut is telling me that he is right. We're here for a reason, and that's not to be tourists. We need to hide. We need to stay safe, if we want to survive. And yet, my body is screaming for the solace of the woods and the shade of trees, if only just for a few moments. I can't be locked up any longer. I feel like I'm going crazy.

I sigh. If I share any of this with him, I doubt he would understand. He is just too practical. I doubt he ever does anything just because he feels like doing it. No. There has to be a good reason behind it. In a way, he is a lot like my dad.

This is why I know I'll require a different strategy, and this one comes from my mom. You simply give your opponent two options, both of which are actually what you want, and you let your opponent choose the one he or she wants. The end result is the same - you get exactly what you wanted, but this way, your opponent feels like they were in control the whole time. This of course, isn't true, but it doesn't matter, does it?

"I suppose you leave me with no other choice, then," I sigh sadly.

I know what he's expecting me to say now. He thinks I'll say that I'll just go back inside, and do as I'm told. Actually, do as I'm told by him. He's probably used to giving out orders, but I'm not really all that used to taking them.

"You will either accompany me now for a brisk walk not too far away from here, or you'll risk me going alone then very soon," I say, with such defiance I never thought I'd find inside of me, especially not under these circumstances.

But, it's true. It's just a walk. And, what can happen if we're safe here?

The shock on his face is priceless. This is one of those rare, precious moments you feel bad you don't have a Polaroid camera with you, so you can take a photo and always remember it. His lips are slightly parted, his eyes wide with disbelief. He never saw it coming, or even expected it of me. Then, against all my expectations, he smiles broadly.

"So, you're blackmailing me now?" I see the corners of his lips dancing, and I want to see more of it.

"It's just an invitation for a quick walk," I shrug, pretending to be all indifferent, but in fact, my heart is pounding so wildly that I feel it'll jump right out of my chest. "You kinda forced me to put it this way."

"I see," he nods, his body leaning a bit backwards, as if to give me a good once over, to make sure it's really me, being all ballsy and confident.

Once he's sure it really is me, he pulls back closer again.

"You don't want me to go alone there, do you?" I ask again.

"Of course not."

"Then, join me for a walk," I urge him. "We're safe here."

"We're not safe anywhere," he corrects me.

"Alright," I snort. "Then, we're safer here than anywhere else in the world. Is that correct?"

I see the hesitation on his face. He wants me to believe that this is the safest place for us, but he won't say it with certainty. I doubt there is anything certain in his world, expect for maybe death, and as Benjamin Franklin said it, taxes. Instead of saying anything, he just nods gently.

"Anderson is taking a nap," I continue. "He won't even know we're gone. And, besides, it's not like we'll be going too far away. We'll be just around the bend. If he calls out to us, for whatever reason, we'd still be able to hear him and rush back."

He seems to ponder the idea for a little while. I smile at him, hoping that will induce his confirmation. He looks around. I can see his nostrils flaring, as if he's sniffing the air around us. I wonder how that feels, to be able to foretell someone's presence, merely based on their odor. For a moment, I feel a little self-conscious. It's not like we have regular baths or showers here, so we all must have an unpleasant body odor. I instantly press my arms to my body, in a futile effort to prevent my glands from spreading my scent all around me. I'm not sure if he noticed it, but he turns to me and smiles.

"The coast seems clear," he tells me, but there is still hesitation in his voice.

"Does that mean what I think it means?"

"But, just a quick walk," he reminds me. "We shouldn't get far away, in case Anderson needs us."

"He's snoring away, I doubt he'll even notice we're missing," I assure him, but he doesn't seem convinced. "I know he probably tells you this often, but you need to relax a little."

"It goes against my character," he says, and I almost miss the joke.

"You didn't just joke there, did you?" I pretend to be all shocked, with my eyes wide opened in mock disbelief.

"Who knows," he shrugs.

We start walking together, our feet synchronizing their steps. We pass through a small, narrow path, which leads us away from our hideout, but still in plain sight of it.

"So, how did you find this place?" I wonder, as we're walking.

"I was running away from some hunters," he explains. "I was still in my wolf form."

I try to imagine him as a wild animal. Untamed. Free. Fearless. I turn to him, and realize that this is exactly how he is even as a human. There is little difference in his behavior. Probably some difference in body hair.

"I was bleeding," he continues. "One of the hunters shot me. I still have a scar on my shoulder. I rushed through the thick bushes, and I found a little hole. It was barely an entrance. But, I knew I couldn't run any longer. I had to hide. Or risk being caught and killed."

"Did they know you were a shifter?"

"I doubt it," he explains. "They just wanted a hunting trophy. I doubt they even took a good long look at me through the barrel of that gun."

"How long did you stay here?"

"I remember being knocked out. So exhausted I didn't even care whether they'd find me or not. I just wanted to sleep. So, I did. When I woke up, I could hear the birds singing outside. I looked down at my body. I had shifted during the night, didn't even feel it. My wound was luckily only surface. It looked much worse than it was. So, I stayed here until I healed properly. But, I did decide to keep this place as my own."

"Weren't you afraid someone might find it?"

I feel like we're going around in a small circle, but I don't mind. It feels nice just to be outside, to walk, pretending if only for a short while that everything's alright. And, the fact that it's Fynn next to me and not Anderson, adds to the strangeness and curiosity of the moment. I dare not look at him while he's talking. Instead, my gaze is fixated on the little path ahead.

"At first, yes. But, after about 10 years had passed, and I hadn't seen a living soul around here, I relaxed a little. Started bringing more stuff here. Spending more time here, as well. It became home in a way."

"Were you... alone?"

The thought of him sleeping there, hurt and without anyone to take care of him, makes me sad. Sadder than I thought it would.

"I've spent a large part of my life alone," he continues. "Then, I met Anderson, and things changed."

"How did you know that he's... well, the same thing you are?" I ask, as I step on a little branch, and it breaks underneath the weight of my foot.

"A shifter?" he smirks. "You just know."

I know what he means, but the feeling of that knowledge eludes me. Sure, I have my gut feeling, but that's far from his ability to smell someone from a mile away.

"How are you doing?" he suddenly asks, and at first, I'm not even sure what exactly he means, as so many things have happened lately, that I was barely able to keep track of all of them.

"Me?" I'm still taken aback by his question, and I almost stumble over a root that protrudes from the ground, but I manage to keep myself balanced. He just nods. "I'm... confused, I guess. And, my dad..."

"I know what I said was harsh."

This time, I stop, and turn to him. My fingers are trembling. We are surrounded by a thick row of bushes and trees, hidden from the world. Maybe here, we can be who we are, without any fear of judgment.

"You told the truth." My lips tremble as I speak.

He takes a step closer to me. The air around us is warm, and it's only getting warmer. I swallow heavily, my lips dry.

"I'm not very good with words," he explains, not that any such explanation is necessary. "But, hope can be a devastating thing sometimes."

The tone of his voice tells me that he probably had a lot of hope at one time, but it was probably dashed, and now, he's afraid to hope for anything. My heart aches. Being hopeless is an immeasurable sadness. I should know.

I lower my gaze, and somehow, I know that we both understand each other. Optimism is a great thing, but sometimes, hope turns out to be your enemy.

"I remember when my mom died," I suddenly start, surprised at the fact that I'm talking about this. Endless hours of therapy sessions with numerous shrinks barely made me talk about this, and here I am, opening up to someone who was mere weeks ago, a complete stranger to me. "I'd spend days in the house, just looking at the door, hoping she'd come in, even though the rational part of my brain knew she would never walk through that door again, and yet, I still hoped. It was a hope that was keeping me buried alive."

I swallow a moan, and quickly wipe a stray tear from my left eye. Some wounds never heal. I know Fynn is equally aware of this.

"That's why I didn't want to feed any false hopes," he tells me. "About - "

"My dad," I nod. "I know. I appreciate that."

"That's why it's great to have someone like Anderson around. He counteracts my negativity with his positivism."

"Yeah," I chuckle. "In a way, you two are the perfect man."

He looks at me, then bursts out into roaring laughter. I join in immediately, and it takes us both a while to calm down. With still a few left-over giggles, we continue on urr way, and shortly after we're back where we started from.

"See?" I smile. "We're back and nothing's happened."

I spread my arms wide, like spreading my wings, as if to prove my point.

"I see," he nods. He quickly glances at his watch.

"Everything OK?"

"Yeah. It's just time to wake up Anderson. It's his turn to take over."

"Do you want me to go wake him up?" I ask.

"No, you stay here," he replies. "It'll be dark soon and you'll have to come back inside anyway. Enjoy the fresh air some more."

"Alright then, I will," I smile, as I take him up on his offer.

"Just, don't stray, alright?" He gestures at me to stay put, and I nod.

I see him go inside, and I turn away to face the greenery around me. As it's getting dark, I can feel the chill. I rub my upper arms with the opposite hand. The air is still, but every once in a while, a breeze blows right through me, chilling me to my very bones, like a premonition.

I wonder what is going to happen. I wonder when, and if, I will ever get my life back. I suppose this can't last forever. Nothing lasts forever. Not good things, not bad things. It's a soothing thought really.

"Maddie!" I hear Fynn shout, and I immediately turn around.

He looks distraught. There is a look on his face, one I would never attribute to him. It's cold, relentless fear. His lips are slightly parted, and I can hear his heavy breath, as it is let out into the world.

"I know this must sound stupid," he starts, pausing for a moment, "but, have you seen Anderson? Has he mentioned going anywhere?"

"I..." His question catches me off guard, and for a moment, I don't know what to say. "I don't know.... I... no... he hasn't said anything. I saw him sleeping, and then I went out to you. Why? What's happened?"

The sound of my own voice frightens me. The look on his face frightens me. My skin has broken out into goosebumps, and all of a sudden, it's gotten much colder.

"Anderson..." he mutters. "Anderson is gone."

Chapter 19

F ynn's words are still ringing in my ear, like an echo of some old song, which your mind refuses to shut out.

Anderson is gone.

I watch as Fynn checks the nearby area, but when he returns with the same forlorn look on his face, I know everything. His silence says it all.

He sighs heavily, like the weight of the world is upon his back. And, it truly is. We are stuck in some God forsaken limbo, with no hope of rectifying this situation. I want to turn to him and ask him what we are going to do now, but I'm scared what the answer might be. I'm petrified that he will tell me the same words that are ringing inside my mind. A bell of three words: I don't know.

I try to breathe deeply, to calm myself down, but it's impossible. Anderson is missing. He wouldn't have gone on his own, without telling us. So, someone must have taken him. And, if someone had taken him, that means that our enemies know exactly where we are, and they are just toying with us. Watching us.

The thought of being watched stifles a scream deep inside my throat. My heart is beating wildly, and no thought can calm it down. A voice inside my mind tells me it's all over. We're done for. They know our every move, and are always two steps ahead.

Suddenly, I break down into tears. He turns to me, but doesn't try to hug me.

"Why are you crying?"

"It's all my fault," I snivel, wiping my eyes with my sleeves.

I look at him, and I see the confusion on his face. He knows I'm right. I suggested that damned walk, and maybe, if all of us had been there, Anderson wouldn't have been taken. Maybe we could have prevented this. And now, Fynn is trying to find a way to be polite about this.

"I know you feel guilty," he starts. "I know that feeling. It can eat you up on the inside, until there is nothing left. Don't do this to yourself."

"How can I not?" I cry out, feeling actual pain in my chest.

"Feeling guilty doesn't change anything. Your crying doesn't change what happened."

"I know, but I can't stop..."

He walks over to me, a little clumsily, my field of vision still a little blurry from all the tears streaming down my face. I see his elbows jerk upward, then fall back down, as if there was a string pulling them back towards his body. A moment later, he tries the motion again, and this time, his elbows remain in the air. His lower arms follow, slowly, gently.

Suddenly, his hands are resting softly on my back, and my face nestles into the soft flesh of his neck. A few left-over sobs escape my chest, and he presses me into him even closer. I inhale deeply, smelling moss and deep woods. My hands clutch at his shoulders, but I'm not crying any longer. Even the sobs have subsided. My body has calmed down.

We remain like that for a few moments longer, neither of us wishing to break free. In that one moment, I forgot all about Anderson being gone. I could have easily swayed myself into believing that he was still asleep inside. However, reality never goes away for a long time. It allows hope to creep in, only long enough to lull you into a false sense of security.

Not knowing how long we stayed like that, I start to let go, and he does the same. I smile at him, blushing, and he takes an even clumsier step backwards. I want to tell him that this was exactly what I needed, but I fear that might make him more self-conscious, so I remain quiet.

His eyes take on a darker hue somehow, and I know that he isn't in this comforting mood any longer. He is back to his usual self.

"Come," he suddenly says and grabs me by the hand.

We rush back inside, and start rummaging through those black bags he warned Anderson and me against. I watch him as he extracts small handguns, and a whole boatload of ammo. His hands work fast, placing everything carefully on the ground in front of him.

He is done surprisingly quickly. He kicks the empty black bags to the side, and looms over the weapons arrangement with his hands firmly on his hips.

"Have you ever used one of these?" he asks, without taking his eyes off of the guns.

My eyes travel over each single weapon, their metallic gleam soft, but visible. Suddenly, a memory floods my mind. I was about four or five years old, and I remember wanting my dad to play with me. My mom was busy in the kitchen, so she just told me to knock on the door to dad's study, and ask him. Only, I didn't knock. My little hand pressed on the doorknob skillfully, with the curiosity and strength only a toddler has, and I barged into my father's study. I remember him being over at his safe, tucked neatly in the corner of the room, behind a wall of tapestry, and a potted plant. There were some papers inside, a few wads of cash, and something metallic. When he saw me, he seemed anxious, confused, as if he was caught doing something he wasn't supposed to be doing. He quickly slammed the safe shut, twisted the knob, and then walked over to me.

"Did you see what daddy has there in his safe?" he asked me, in his your-my-big-girl voice. I just shook my head to that. I wasn't lying, but at the same time, I also wasn't telling the truth. I was somewhere in what I considered to be a safe place between. "Those are daddy's things in there, OK, pumpkin? It's always locked and it needs to stay that way. If you ever see it open, come find me immediately, without touching anything there, OK?"

My curiosity peaked at that very moment, but even as a toddler I knew that he wouldn't show me what's inside. So, I just nodded again, and allowed him to hug me, my little arms wrapped around his meaty neck.

"No, never," I tell Fynn, my child's mind reminding me that I did see one of those, in my own home, but luckily, I was never forced to use it.

"Here," he bends down and picks up the smallest gun from the bundle. "Look here."

He opens the gun, clicks it, twists it, all I hear are metallic clicks and clanks. Then, he points it away from us.

"You just pull the trigger and shoot. First shoot, ask questions later, got it?" He sounds out of breath, like he's been running for hours before this.

He hands it to me, like one hands the latest newspaper off the stand, and not a gun. I hesitate to take it and he notices.

"Are you scared?" he asks.

"Mhm," I muster.

It's not the gun that scares me. Holding it in my hand and feeling its hard surface doesn't make me afraid. The knowledge that I'd have to pull that trigger does. Because, I'm sure Fynn wouldn't be handing it to me unless he expects me to use it.

"We have two options," he tells me, that gun still between us, lingering in the air. He isn't pulling it back, and I'm not taking it. "Fight or flee."

I know what his choice is. It's evident. But, that fear that has my feet nailed to the ground doesn't agree.

"It makes no sense," I shake my head in disbelief. "It's only the two of us. Who knows how many there are of them."

"Maddie, there is nowhere else to go," I hear hopelessness in his voice and I know he is telling me the truth. "This was the last place on Earth I thought we'd be safe. I was wrong. And, now they have my partner."

"Do you think he's…" I start, but he cuts me off.

"No!" His voice thunders. "I'm gonna find him. We are gonna find him."

It's strange to hear him talk like this. But, I understand.

"I can drive you somewhere else, but honestly, I don't even know where. I doubt I could protect you anywhere else by hiding you. The best I can do is fight until my last breath to keep you safe and unharmed."

The thought of him fighting a small army of wolf shifters or maybe something even worse frightens me to death. But, I know that's a possibility. My heart is beating in my throat, threatening to jump right out of my chest. I look at him straight in the eyes, and grab the gun from his hand. The gun seems inadequate in my trembling hand, and I have no idea if I'll dare to pull the trigger when the time comes. But, I can't dwell on that right now. I need to believe that I can and I will. Fynn needs me. I can't let him down. I can't let Anderson down.

"Things are in perspective now," I exhale loudly.

"Yes," he nods. "You see now we can't flee. That instinct telling you to run? That's prey instinct. And we aren't prey."

I listen to him talk, and I can almost imagine myself running barefoot through the woods. He lights up a fire inside of me, a strength I never knew I possessed. I'm no longer a scared little girl. I am a warrior. And, they will not have me without a fight.

"We stay here," he continues. "We fight. That's what warriors do. That is what hunters do. We will kill all of those who come for us. We will fight and be saved, and then, we will go find Anderson."

His hand caged mine, the one holding the gun. I could feel the power of his being surging through me. It was, as if, in the strangest of ways, we've connected. We've become one. He has taken over some of my weakness and in its place, left his own strength to protect me, to guide me.

"You can do this," he tells me again, knowing I need to hear it over and over again. "Now, let's go outside to set up the traps."

I nod, following him through the door. But, the moment, we exit, we see it immediately, at the same time. There is a note stuck to our door, held in place by a little pocket knife.

The Boon.

Tomorrow at 9 pm.

Bring the girl if you ever want to find out what happened to Hugo.

S.

Fynn pulls it off the door forcefully, then crumples up the paper. They're playing with us. They've been playing with us all this time, and we've fallen right into their trap.

I look over at Fynn. His nostrils are flaring. His nose is raised high up in the air, but I doubt he'll pick up on anything. They're long gone. Left to laugh at us, waiting for us to keep playing their game.

Chapter 20

Anderson
When I wake up, I feel like there is a whole orchestra playing inside my head. Looking too much to the left hurts. Come to think of it, looking any way other than straight ahead fucking hurts. I try to move my arms, and only then do I realize that I'm sitting on a chair, which I'm also tied to. I try the ropes, but they're too tight. The more I struggle, the more they dig into my flesh.

I look around, and the moment I do that, a flicker of a small light appears in the darkest corner.

"Well, look who's awake."

It's a voice I'd recognize anywhere. Only snakes hiss like that.

Sven's cigarette intensifies the flame, and he walks out into the light. It barely illuminates anything, but I can see him. The first thing I notice is the scar, then the rest of him.

I try to remember what happened, but it's all a blur. I remember sleeping in the bed, then some commotion. Someone's hand over my mouth. Some sweet-smelling liquid pressed to my nose and lips.

"You fucking drugged me!" I growl at him, shaking the chair, in a futile effort to get loose and lunge at him.

He just chuckles. "Save your strength. You'll need it for when your friends arrive."

"You motherfucker! What have you done to them?"

"Nothing yet," he tells me, shaking his head in his usual, calm manner. He'd make you almost believe that he's just here to talk, and then he slits your throat while you're not looking. "They're not even here. We're expecting them in a few hours, though."

"What do you want?" I ask, even though I know he probably won't answer.

"All questions will be answered in due time," he assures me, inhaling deeply, then releasing a long, satisfying breath of smoke. "But, Hugo wouldn't tell us where it is."

"Where what is!?"

Sven shakes his head in disapproval. He walks over to me, then without a single word, presses the burning end of the cigarette on the bare skin of my hand.

"Aaaaaaaaargh!" I scream at the top of my lungs, as it burns through my flesh. "You fucker!"

He pulls it away, as the small red circle remains, reminding me of his anger. But, there's more of it to come. I know it.

I breathe heavily, as the pain subsides.

"It was with Hugo," Sven continues. "We know it was in his safe. The problem is that it's not there anymore, and Hugo... well, let's just say Hugo isn't talking anymore."

"Is he... dead?"

"That's part of the surprise. And, I can't ruin the surprise."

"What surprise?"

"Didn't I just say I can't ruin it?" he chuckles again, finishing the cigarette, then stomping on it with his foot.

"Why don't you just kill me and get it over with?" I growl at him again, angered that they took me out so easily.

Then, it hits me. If they went inside our hideout, where was Fynn? Wasn't he supposed to be watching the place? What was he doing?

"It's more fun this way," he tells me. "Besides, there is a point to all this. You'll see. Also, I'm told not to harm you. At least not until we wrap this up properly. Then, my hands get untied and I go crazy!"

He doesn't need to say that twice. No one wants to be around when Sven is allowed, and actually encouraged, to go crazy. All I can hope for is that Fynn won't be enough of a fool to actually come here on his own, looking for me.

I shake the chair a little more, but I know there's no point. Sven doesn't make such mistakes of using wobbly chairs or tying up his victims loosely. He's way too meticulous for that.

"Like I said, you should save your strength for later," he reminds me.

"You won't get away with this."

This sounds like some cheesy, worn out line from a movie, but at the moment, that's all I can come up with. And, Sven knows it. He just stares at me, then bends down, hands on his knees, and starts laughing his ass off. He laughs for a while like that, the whole place echoing, then he finally straightens.

"That one was really good, Anderson. Got any more cliché movie lines?"

I don't grace that with a reply.

"Silence?" he wonders. "Alright. I grow tired of this anyway. I'm just supposed to watch you until you wake up. Then, one of the thugs takes over. I've got business to attend to."

He heads over to the door, slamming it shut after him. My mind races, as I look around, trying to find something to use as a means of escape. It's a big, empty room. Probably used to be the boiler room, as there are several pipes still hanging from the ceiling and from the walls. The floor has been stripped of any flooring. It's bare cement now.

I look at the chair. Pretty sturdy, with strong legs and back. The rope is tight, double knotted. If I had been awake while they were tying me up, I would have remembered to inhale deeply and enlarge my frame, which could have made wriggling out of these ropes easier. Now, they're tightly wound around me.

Fuck. Fuck. I have to wait for the first opportunity to get free. Only how?

At that moment, the door opens, and an unfamiliar face walks in. It's swollen from too much alcohol and drugs, probably. The guy is dressed all in black, and he doesn't walk over to me. He just stops by the door and crosses his arms in front of his chest, giving me an orangutan look.

Now I get it. He's the thug. Thugs usually don't talk. They just beat the crap out of you.

I exhale loudly. This guy probably has instructions not to get near me, not to talk to me, not even to acknowledge me. But, I know a way he'd be forced to get near me.

I inhale deeply once more, preparing myself for the pain that's about to follow. But, I can't wait for Sven to return and find me in the same spot. I might not get up from this chair alive.

I remember the last time I was out of breath. It was a particularly dangerous mission, during which Fynn and I got separated. I was the first to stumble onto our target, only no one told us that the guy was a fucking bear shifter with hands the size of a football. He grabbed me by the neck and shoved me against the wall, pressing hard. At one point, I saw stars. Just darkness, with tiny freckles of light, and I thought I was a goner. Fynn smashed a brick on the guy's head, and knocked him out cold. Needless to say, it took me a while to start talking properly again after that.

But, that is what I need to do now. Put on a show. The fucking show of my life.

I start coughing at first, expelling more air than I take in, to make it more believable. The guy turns to look at me curiously, but he doesn't budge. Still. I start taking short, wheezy breaths, again expelling more air out of my lungs, purposefully making myself suffocate, or at least sound like I'm suffocating. I tighten my jaw, then open my mouth wide. I try to envision those same hands around my neck, and surprisingly, it's not that hard. I guess you never forget some things.

"My.... inhaler...." I wheeze at the guy in the corner. "Can't.... breeeeeeathe..."

And, with those words I let my head flop down towards my chest. I make sure to keep my eyes closed, and my ears pricked up. When one of your senses is off, then others become much keener than normal. Seeing I was left with barely anything functional in my nose, that meant that I needed to focus on my hearing. Now, it is paying off more than ever.

I hear the guy's footsteps moving closer and closer to me. If my nose was any good, I'd be able to tell exactly when he's in front of me, or when he leans down to check on me. But, I can't smell him. Instead, I can only listen. His body fights the air around him, the air that is in this case, my best friend. He's a heavy guy, his shoes are pressing hard against the cement floor, even though the soles of his shoes try to soak up all the noise. But, it's impossible. A keen ear will always hear them.

Making sure to breathe as slowly as possible, I need to confuse him. I need to make him think that I'm dying. I'm on the verge of death, and he needs to find my non-existent inhaler.

I hear him stop a little away from me. He hesitates to approach me. My breathing has calmed down to the extent of being barely noticeable. Suddenly, I feel his fingers pressing against my jeans pockets. He feels nothing. He checks the pockets of my jacket, and I feel a gush of air brought on by his presence.

I know this is my moment. It's now or never.

I lift my head as hard as I can, and I come down onto his with a bang. A million sharp needles of pain pierce through my face, my forehead and my chin. I try not to focus on the nerve-wracking pain, because I know there will be more to follow. The thug's body slumps down onto the floor, right in front of me. A thin trickle of blood starts oozing from both of his nostrils. But, I know such a big guy won't stay down so easily. So, I need to go on with my plan.

I look down at my legs. They're both tied to the chair legs. My hands are tied to my back. The only way I can do this is the most painful. But, I can't risk this guy getting up, or Sven coming back. I need to do this now.

I take another deep breath, trying to tighten my muscles as much as possible. The wall is close behind me. I just need to bang against it as hard as I can. Slowly, I lower my body onto my feet, managing to keep a balance of both my body and the chair that's tied to my back. Without thinking, as these things usually go, I slam hard backwards, as hard as I can. A part of the chair breaks, but the seat and the legs remain intact. I sway to the front again, and repeat the action, even harder this time, ready for any stray spike that might dig into me. But, at this point, it's a risk I'm willing to take.

Sometimes, you got more luck than brains, and this is exactly one of those situations. The back of the chair separates and my hands are loosened. I manage to wiggle them free of the rope, and I do the same with my legs.

As I'm about to step over the body which lies prostrate on the floor, I feel the guy's hand grab at my ankle. With one swift kick in the chin, I solve that problem. His head jerks to the other side, and I stay there another moment, to see if he's getting up again. Once I'm sure that he's knocked out for good, I step over him and walk to the door.

I expect it to be locked. But, again - more luck than brains. I smile at the silver lining in this whole shit storm, and push the door open. A dark hallway opens up before me. I can't see shit in there. I hear nothing but silence. Fynn's nose would come in mighty handy now, but who knows where he is.

I wonder if he and Maddie are alright. If she's with him, she should be. He'd die first before letting anything happen to her. I know it. So, maybe I shouldn't worry about them. I should worry about myself.

With positivity in mind, I take a step down the dark hallway, hoping that whatever monster is lurking in its depths would be one I can take on.

Chapter 21

"You can't come and that's final!" Fynn growls at me, as he shoves his gun in the back of his pants, then adjusts his shirt over it.

"But, you said you needed me," I snort. "Why would you give me a gun then?"

"Because I thought they'd come after us here," he explains. "Then, we would have been able to set up traps, and stay inside. We might have been able to take them on, just the two of us, because they'd come to us, on our terrain. Instead, they turned the tables on us."

He sighs heavily as he speaks, his forehead all wrinkled and brows furrowed. This is the Fynn that I've known from day one. Serious Fynn. Fynn who always solves problems. Fynn who doesn't sugar coat things.

"I know you're scared that something will happen to me," I start. "I'm scared of that, too."

"That's why I need to take you somewhere, where you can hide," he interrupts me.

"But, you've said it yourself. There is nowhere else to hide."

"That's why it doesn't matter where you go. Any place will do. They won't know where you are, because we don't know where to go, where to take you."

"Stop talking in riddles!" I feel myself getting angry at him, and that's the last thing I want. He's on my side. We're on the same team, and we need to work together to survive, to find Anderson.

"Just let me come with you," I plead.

"I can't do that," he shakes his head.

"I can help you."

"You'll be a distraction," he snorts, not caring the least bit that he might hurt my feelings. He just tells it like it is, and you need to deal with it, if you want to go along for the ride. "I can't focus on finding Anderson and trying to keep you alive."

"I can do that just fine on my own," I sneer. Of course I know that's not true, but the heat of the moment is high, and I'll say anything to have him take me along. "And, besides, I need to find out what happened to my father, Fynn. This isn't just about you and Anderson, you know."

He doesn't immediately reply to that. He gives it some thought, and I want to open his brain to see what's going on inside.

"They only added that to the message to make sure you'll come, so they can end it all easily, and not go hunting you down after they're done with me and Anderson."

The thought of us all dying makes my blood turn cold. But, it's a real possibility. A tangible reality. I know why he doesn't want me to go along. He wants me away, as safe as I can be under the circumstances. What he doesn't realize is that without my father, without the two of them, I have nothing. I'm all alone in this world.

"Never underestimate someone who has nothing to lose," I tell him. "I know they want me to come. And, I'll be happy to oblige."

Fynn sighs. "There is no talking you out of it, is there?"

"No," I shake my head.

The breeze blows through my hair, ruffling it a little. It reminds me how cold and heartless life can get. I thought I lived through the worst tragedy of my life when I lost my mother. Now, it turns out I might have to go through all of it again, and even worse. Face being left completely alone in the world.

"This is a horrible idea," he rolls his eyes. "Let's just be clear on that."

"We are."

"But, if I don't take you with me, you'll follow me or something, and still end up there, right?"

"Right." I can't help but smile. "See? You know me so well."

"I know that you really don't like taking orders."

"When I agree with them, sure. I'll listen."

"But sometimes, others know better. Why can't you listen then?" he asks and I don't know what to tell him.

"I need to find out what happened to my father," I keep on telling him the only thing that matters right now. "I need to see if he's alive or dead. Maybe... maybe that bullet didn't hit him. Maybe he's just wounded. Maybe he's waiting for me, for us, to come and rescue him. I can't leave him. Not like our mother was left."

"Maddie..." He walks over to me. "I know you're confused about your mother's death. Anderson shouldn't have been the one to tell you anything. Even though it seems that if he hadn't, then Hugo wouldn't have the chance up to this point. So, maybe it's good Anderson took it upon himself. But, it's not Hugo's fault. Your father is a decent guy. Always has been. He just got caught up in some shady things, and unfortunately... your mother ended up paying the price for it."

I swallow heavily. My mother is the last thing I want to talk about right now, but I can't say anything. I'm just focusing on not crying. I want my old photo album, so I can take just one look at her smiling face. But, I can't. I don't even know if I'll ever be able to return to the house I once called my home. Will I even find all my stuff there or has Sven already stormed through the place?

"Your father needs your forgiveness, more than anything," Fynn says.

"I don't even know if he's alive."

He sighs. "I don't ever do this," he clears his throat a little, "but, what is your heart telling you?"

I look at him, puzzled.

"Close your eyes," he instructs me, putting his hands on my shoulder. His touch is electrifying. I notice that he's done it much more easily this time. My body relaxes. "Picture your father with the eye of your mind. Can you see him?"

"Mhm," I nod, my eyes still closed.

"What is he doing?"

"He is... reading in his study," I actually smile at this mental image. "I barged into the room, but he is never upset when I do this. Not once."

"Looking at him like that, what is your heart telling you?"

I suddenly open my eyes. I can't believe he, of all people, is asking me that question. But, I reply.

"He's still alive," I whisper, my whole body trembling.

"Then, we'll find him," he nods. "I promise you that."

He quickly takes his hands off of me, and I feel like he just electrocuted me. I'm still shaking, barely able to keep my balance. Fear washes over me. What if I can't do this?

"You still have that gun I gave you?"

"Mhm."

"Good. You'll take this one as well. And, here's some ammo. I'll show you how to load them."

He turns away and grabs a few small bags in his hand.

"Fynn?" I lower my eyelids.

"Yes?"

"Do you think we can do this?"

"If you want some assurances that we will all get out unharmed from this, I'm afraid I can't give you that. I'm not sure of anything right now. All I'm sure of is that there is a sky over us and there is ground beneath us. Those are the only two things I know. The rest is all up for discussion."

I don't say anything to that. There's nothing to say really. But, his words fill me with a strange sense of awe. There are so many possibilities, and in one of them, maybe even many of them, we do get out of this whole ordeal unharmed and alive. That's all I need to remember.

"Now, let me show you how to use this gun," he urges me to come over and I do so.

A few hours later, we're at the designated location. Fynn had explained to me that the Boon was an old tavern, which was torn down ages ago, and all that is left of it are just four big walls and a roof that's about to collapse any minute now.

Fynn parks the car a bit away, but I doubt anything we do would give us the surprise advantage. We already lost that.

We get out of the car, and I look around. We're on the outskirts of the city. It's closed off, secluded. There is no traffic of any kind around. If you want to do anything illegal, this would be your place to do it.

"You OK?" Fynn asks me, as he checks the guns on him.

He bends down to one knee, and lifts his trouser leg. I see the glimmer of a small knife in a pocket around his ankle. He adjusts it, then gets back up.

"I'm fine," I nod.

I'm everything but fine, but is there a point in reporting that? I need to convince myself that I'm fine, that I can do this. Whatever this is. First I was running away from my kidnapper, and now, I'm walking straight towards him.

"Just stay close," he whispers, then heads on first.

He is walking slowly, his body is slumping forward. I can barely hear his footsteps. I try to be as stealthy as he is, but it's difficult. I step on a dry branch, or on some rubble which grinds underneath the soles of my shoes. Fynn doesn't say anything. He just keeps on going, his hand constantly pressed to his side, where his gun is. Mine is already in my trembling hand, as I wonder whether I'll have the guts to pull the trigger.

Something rustles in the bushes nearby, and we both jump. He sniffs the air, then shakes his head.

"A squirrel."

I'm so nervous I'm about to burst out into loud laughter, but I manage to calm myself down. We finally reach what looks like a door, hanging off its hinges. Fynn looks around, but apart from a few flickering lights in the distance, it looks like we're the only ones here.

"Please, relinquish your weapons."

We suddenly hear a voice from behind us, and a cocking of a gun, which sounded much bigger than either of ours.

"I always wanted to say it so dramatically."

I don't need to turn around to recognize that voice.

"Throw your gun to the ground," Fynn instructs me and I do it.

"You can turn around now," Sven tells us.

He is standing there with a bodyguard to the left and right of him.

"It's a pleasure to see you again, Miss Holloway," he tells me. "And, of course, Fynn. Not such a pleasure, right?" He laughs at his own joke, and the two guys next to him chuckle silently. "If you would be so kind as to follow me inside."

The guards rush over to get our weapons from us, and they search both of us.

"Hey!" I shout, trying to push him away, as he presses his hands on my breasts.

"Bear, don't be so hard with the girl," Sven shakes his head. "On second thought, maybe I should do it. You know I've got the softer touch."

He walks over to me, while Bear stands next to Fynn.

"This is just a precaution, my dear," Sven starts.

His fingers grab me by the neck, but they don't squeeze. He rakes them through my hair, probably to see if I'm hiding anything there. Then, the tips of his fingers trace lines down my back, and he is so close to me that our faces are almost touching. I turn my face away, to the side, and he grins.

"We don't want you pulling a little handgun or something in the most awkward moment, now do we?"

His hands then cup my breasts, but I don't say anything.

"Get your fucking hands off her!" I hear Fynn thunder.

He tries to lunge at Sven, but the two guards hold him back. Sven turns to him.

"Oh, I apologize. Does she belong to you?" he asks. "Has she been claimed already?"

"Claimed?" I repeat, wanting to spit right in his face, but I resist the urge. It would only make him angry, and that's not what I want.

"Every shifter needs a mate," Sven explains. "Someone to prolong the special race, you see. And, she has to be very..." he pauses to get so close to me that he inhales deeply the scent of my hair and neck, "special."

He exhales loudly, and the grip he had on my breasts loosens. He goes over my waist, inner and outer thighs and then stops.

"I must say, Fynn, she is a fine choice. A fine choice indeed. But, is daddy dearest in agreement with this?"

"Fuck you," Fynn growls.

"All in due time," Sven grins. "I also might include your trophy here in that endeavor."

He cups my chin with his fingers, and I jerk away from him.

"She's got spunk. You gotta love that in a woman," Sven looks over at his guards, and they all start laughing.

I look over at Fynn, helpless. I see the rage in his eyes. But, I also see that he has a plan. I can't be sure of it, but it's a gut feeling, and if anything, I've learned to trust my gut feeling over the years.

"Alright, now that the fun is over, we can continue with the matter at hand," Sven informs us. "Take them inside."

We are then led inside the old, forgotten tavern, and the darkness that opens up before me is frightening. But, not as much as what I fear I might find inside of it.

Chapter 22

F ynn

We're brought into a small room. It's dusty and dirty. There is no furniture apart from some old, broken down piano with a layer of cobwebs on it. Two chairs are brought in, and we're tied to them. I curse silently at myself, for not telling her about this. I take a deep breath as the big thug wraps a thick rope around me, and tries to tighten it as much as he can. I've been tied up more times than I can count, so this isn't new to me.

I watch as she does exactly the opposite. Maddie cowers. She makes herself as small as possible. Her body comes into itself, and it's easy to entangle her so hard that I doubt she'd ever get out of those ropes without some help. As for me, I might. But, I need to bide my time.

When the rope welcome is over, the thugs move to the side, giving Sven the spotlight.

He takes one of his cigarettes and lights it up.

"You know those'll kill you?" I frown at him.

"They've been trying for decades," Sven replies. "Still no luck."

He walks over to me and brings it to my lips. It's one of those expensive, Cuban cigarettes. The ones you have to kill for to get a box. I remember those. I turn away.

"I'm trying to quit."

"Too bad," he shakes his head. "It might be your last one."

"So, are you finally going to reveal the big pinnacle of this fucking Shakespearean drama you've got going?" I snort, having had enough of this already.

Also, Sven prides himself on being calm. That's when he's most cruel. But, you get him angry, and you get him careless. That's my plan here.

"The twist is to die for, you'll see," Sven is cracking up at this point.

I look over at Maddie. She's scared. She's so scared that I see tears glistening in her eyes. The thought of her being tied up there, and even more, Sven touching her the way he did, brings me to the edge. I just need one little thing to push me over it.

"But, of course, I'll start explaining," Sven says. "I believe we all know why we targeted little Miss Sunshine over here."

He walks over to Maddie and gives a big kiss on the forehead.

"Fuck you!" she growls at him.

Good girl.

"Real feisty," Sven pinches her cheek. "I can think of a few scenarios where that might come in handy, but I stray. We all know her father, Hugo Holloway. We also know who he owes his vast fortune to."

I'm listening to Sven talk, and I see the confusion on Maddie's face. She knows something, but probably not all. But, from the looks of it, we're both in the dark.

"Do you remember, Fynn?" he asks me.

"Kayne," I reply.

"Exactly!" Sven gives me a mocking applause.

"But, Kayne is dead," I remind him. "He's been dead for 15 years. What the fuck does he have to do with anything now?"

Sven gives me one of those oh-oh looks.

"It seems that someone here hasn't been brought in on the news yet."

"What news?" I snort.

"Kayne is alive."

"The fuck he is," I hiss at him. "I saw him burn in that house with my own eyes."

"Correction," Sven shakes his index finger at me, as the other one is still busy holding his half-finished cigarette. "You saw a house on fire. You saw someone was inside at the start of the fire. But, have you seen his body?"

"He burned."

"He did burn, somewhat, yes. But, you know the wonders of modern medicine. They take a little bit of skin from one part of your body, or from someone else's body, that also works apparently, and they just replace the burned area with new, rejuvenated skin. And, they can also change your profile a little, so you don't look like yourself so much. And, when someone who once knew you sees the new you, they can't even recognize you."

"What the Hell are you jabbering about?" I'm fuming at this point.

If what he's saying is true, than it all makes sense. If Kayne is back, there will be Hell to pay. He'll be out for revenge. For blood. My blood. Anderson's blood. Hugo's blood.

"I still find it funny, you know," Sven chuckles, takes one last satisfying puff of his cigarette, and then throws it onto the cement floor. He doesn't even bother to extinguish it, and it just remains there, flickering powerlessly, until it dies out on its own, without any help. "You couldn't recognize him."

"Recognize who?" I snap at him.

I could tear off these ropes this minute, but that'd be wrong. I'm too strung up, too agitated and angry to think clearly. I'd waste my only chance to actually save Maddie and us with her. I need to calm down. I know what he's doing. He's doing to me what I wanted to do to him. He's walking me along the edge, so that he can push me into it, and then, there will be no going back.

"Me, of course."

I turn to the door, and Maddie does so at the same time. She doesn't recognize the man she sees. How could she? She's never seen Kayne. She's never seen the guy her father made the mistake of doing business with. And, besides, the man who is standing in the doorway looks nothing like Kayne. His cheekbones are slightly higher. His face looks wider. His forehead has a few more wrinkles. His hair is darker, curlier. His lips fuller. But, his eyes. I only notice his eyes now. They're the same. He didn't want to change them, even though he could have easily.

"What are you doing here, Chief?" I ask, feeling as if someone punched all the air out of my lungs.

The question is stupid. But, that's the only thing I can say, even though I know the answer to that. Of course. It makes sense. He's the only one who could have told Sven about the safe house. And, even though I didn't mention my place, he could have tracked us down. Fucking fuck.

"I believe you know my real name now," Kayne tells me.

Now, his real voice surfaces. As Chief, he did his best to change both his appearance and his voice to not resemble Kayne even slightly. Motherfucker did a good job.

The memories of that night flood me. Anderson and I were there, along with a few others from our pack. Kayne needed to be dealt with. We couldn't stand by and take his shit anymore. He was harming everyone. Us. Humans. He was getting worse and we knew there was only one way to stop him.

So, we locked him inside the house and then we set it on fire. I watched the house burn. I was the last one who left the scene. I stepped over the still smoking coals and ashes, to make sure everything burned to the ground. To make sure nothing was left of him.

But, now, here he was. A phoenix rising from the ashes of the past.

"I don't think I need to remind you of that night, Fynn," Kayne continues, reading my mind. "But, our guest here knows nothing about it."

He turns to Maddie. She looks petrified. Why did I let her come with me? Stupid, stupid, stupid. I made the same mistake again. I'll lose her, just like I lose everyone I care about, because I'm too weak to put my foot down.

"You leave her out of it," I order him, but it comes out more as a whine than a growl.

"I can't do that," Kayne shakes his head. "She is the crucial element to my revenge."

"Your revenge?" I ask.

"Don't play dumb!" Kayne hisses at me, his canine teeth bared, ready to dig into my flesh. "But, I'll take care of you later. Hugo is the one I want."

"My father?" Maddie manages to muster, and we all turn to her, as if we're seeing her here for the first time.

Kayne walks over to her, then stands right in front of her. She looks at him straight in the eyes, defiant, even though nothing about her situation allows her this defiance. And, yet, she still stands.

"If you haven't figured it out already, your father and I did some business back in the day," Kayne starts. "I loaned him some money, and he promised to give it back. When he couldn't pay up, I offered another means of payment, just to let me dip into his business and get a little cut of my own for the foreseeable future. But, as you know, he's very selfish about his work, and refused my overly generous offer. Also, there is something he's been holding out on, something I want, something that would sort this all out easily. But, he wouldn't give it to me. Now, all this is just... punishment, I'm afraid. Like the last time."

Maddie's eyes fill with tears, but they aren't tears of sadness. They are tears of rage.

"It was you," she says. "You killed my mother."

"Your mother was just an unfortunate victim of circumstance, I'm afraid," he shrugs. "I had nothing against her. Lovely lady, really. I'm almost sorry for what happened. But, what can you do."

With those words, he turns to me again, but I'm not looking at him. I'm looking at Maddie. Her body is shaking. It starts with the fingers first, then her lower legs. Her head starts to twitch to the left, then to the right.

"Maddie?" I call out to her. "Are you OK?"

She doesn't answer. I'm not even sure she hears me. Instead, she opens her mouth and screams loudly, from the top of her mouth.

"Aaaaaaaaaaaaaaaaargh!"

Her voice pierces through our ears, and I watch as both Sven and Kayne put their hands over their ears.

"Fucking stop her!" Kayne shouts at the guards, one of whom approaches Maddie and starts shaking her wildly, but nothing happens. The scream continues.

The guy steps away, not sure what to do.

"What the fuck are you waiting for!?" Kayne curses. "Smack her! Make her stop somehow!"

The moment one of those big guys is about to raise his hand at Maddie, I know I've crossed over the edge. They pushed me and now, they will face the consequences.

All the muscles in my body tighten, then suddenly relax. The ropes slide downwards a little, and I'm not only able to get my feet out of the ropes, but my hands as well. I rush over to Maddie, and deliver a sucker punch to the guy, which sends him headlong into the opposing wall. The other guy rushes at me immediately, but I turn around in time to see him. I slide to the left, using my right arm to grab him by the neck, and slam his head forcefully into the floor.

Breathing heavily, unfazed by the bleeding bodies on the ground, I stand by Maddie.

"Don't be ridiculous," Kayne shakes his head incredulously at me. "You can't take both of us."

"She can help me," I say, knowing full well how ridiculous that sounds. But, I'm just trying to buy time here.

"She?" Sven answers this time, laughing. "Fine, cut her lose. Let her help you."

I quickly use the time I'm given. As I'm untying Maddie, I bend over to her right ear.

"They didn't take my knife," I tell her, making sure not to move my lips too much. "When I release you, bend down and take it, so they don't see it."

I watch her as she nods, her eyes wide with fear and shock. I wish I could tell her it's alright, that we'll get out of this, but I can't. But, I can hold her hand and promise that we'll go down together.

I almost believe she can read my mind when she takes me by the hand and gets up. She's done it so effortlessly that I didn't even feel her take the knife from my inside trouser leg pocket. I could only hope that she would know to use it when the time came.

"I've had enough of this," Kayne growls, taking a step forward. "This stopped being fun."

I instinctively do the same, protecting Maddie with my body.

"Don't worry, I won't hurt your little girlfriend," Kayne mocks. "I'll just make her watch while I kill you."

"We'll see about that."

As we talk, we start walking around in a circle. I know I can't take both of them, Kayne and Sven. So, if Sven decides to interfere, it's done.

"I think it's high time we end this once and for all," Kayne continues, and I couldn't agree more.

"You should have burned in that house 15 years ago!"

"You motherfucker!" he shouts at me.

We lunge at each other at the same time. It's like waiting for disaster to strike, but there is nothing anyone can do about it. None of us is armed, and that's exactly how we're used to it. My fist dug into Kayne's body, but at the same time, a sudden tidal wave of pain jolted right through me. I almost lost balance. I swayed to the left, but managed to keep myself standing.

Kayne dropped to the ground. He spat out some blood. He was winded. Obviously, he had forgotten what it's like to fight another shifter. Fighting humans is easy. But, fighting those on the same level as you - not so much.

He gives me a grotesque look. A look of hatred. I know neither of us will walk away. I shuffle to the side, waiting for another attack. But, instead of an attack that comes from Kayne, I feel something hard and merciless driven right into my back. The force of that blow is so hard that I drop to my knees, panting.

"Stop!" I hear Maddie scream, but her words are met with disdain and laughter.

There is nothing she can do. And, I can't take both of them at the same time. Maybe back in the day when I was a young shifter, full of strength and bravery, but not now. Not like this.

I feel two pairs of hands trying to overpower me, and I let them. I can't breathe properly still. The after-effects of Sven's blow are still electrifying my body. Now, I know which ones here will be allowed to walk away.

"Hey, bastards!" Suddenly, a familiar voice breaks the silence. "I thought two to one was an unfair fight."

"Anderson!" Maddie is the first to shout his name, like a beacon of light in the darkest moment.

I want to shout his name, too, but I can barely inhale properly, let alone shout. I look over at Sven and Kayne, and I realize that Anderson probably doesn't know what's happening yet.

"Chief?" Anderson is still standing in the doorway, only now recognizing the man I'm fighting as our boss.

"Fynn has betrayed us," Kayne actually tries this.

"Fynn?" Anderson turns to me. I see shock in his eyes. Confusion.

"Don't tell me you really buy this shit?" I use all my strength to spit out these words, and the pain is worth it. Anderson knows me. "Chief is Kayne."

"Kayne?" Anderson cries. "But, he's dead."

"I'm very much alive," Kayne corrects him. "And you two have been fucking up my plan for far too long. I finally got Hugo, but you had to interfere and almost ruin everything."

"What have you done to him?" Anderson shouts. "Where is he?"

"He's where you'll never find him," Kayne replies, with a wicked gleam in his eyes. "And, I'll leave it to your imagination to find out if I left him there alive or dead."

"Oh, no!" Maddie shouts, her hands flying to her face. "My poor dad!"

Everything is out in the open now. This is the reason why we are all here. But, this time, we are going to put an end to it, once and for all.

"Only two shifters will be leaving the Boon tonight," I tell them.

Anderson rushes over to my side, our bodies shielding Maddie. She hides away in the corner. At least, she will be safe there. Until we're done with this scum.

"Bring it on," Sven bares his teeth at us.

I feel it coming on. The pain will be unbearable. It is a death and birth all in one. A rebirth, every single time. I've done it only a handful of times in my life. Only when I was forced to. This time, no one is forcing me. It is my choice. My wish. And I know Anderson feels the same.

It's coming. It's almost here. It'll tear me apart, before it puts me back together again, but this time, it'll be worth it.

Chapter 23

I'm cowering in the corner at what is to happen before me. Not in a million years did I think I'd ever witness something like this. I watch as the two men before me are about to fight their enemies. Our enemies. The knife in my hand shakes. I can't steady it. I doubt I could even use it. I'm overcome by fear at the possible outcome.

I watch as Fynn drops to the ground first. His upper back lunges up into the air, the bones inside his body looking so sharp that they are about to pierce right through his skin and his clothes. He coughs violently, retching silently, but nothing comes out of his mouth. Only air. I look over at Anderson. He's still on his feet, but barely. His fingers are twitching, extending then bending, every muscle in his body awake.

I know what's going to happen. I don't know how, but I know what I'm looking at. Fynn's lower jaw protrudes outward, I see the outlines of his white teeth. Somehow, they elongate, with every subsequent glance, his teeth are larger, longer, and pointier.

Then, the cracking noises begin. At first, I don't know what it is. I look at the doorway, thinking someone's come, but it's still just the five of us in here. And, I know once this is all over, not everyone will walk back out into the sunlight.

I realize that the noises are coming from Fynn and Anderson. Their bones are cracking. They are being rearranged inside of their bodies to accommodate for the new shape that is about to be born.

"Oh, my God!" I gasp silently, pressing my hands to my lips, eyes wide open and unable to look away.

Their bodies start to shape, to enlarge. Different body parts elongate, extend, twist upward or downward in the strangest angles. Cracking noises fill the room. Heavy breathing is all around me.

All of a sudden, little parts of skin start to peel off of their bodies, and I can't watch any longer. I close my eyes, relying solely on my ears to know that they're doing exactly what they should be doing. I breathe heavily, trying to drown out the moans and groans, and after what seems to be a small eternity, I open my eyes again.

The sight before me is terrifying. There are miniature puddles of blood all around us. I see shredded pieces of clothing. Something that looks like a piece of bone protruding from one of the puddles.

I gasp. I don't see four men in front of me any longer. Instead, what I see are four humanoid wolves, their bodies lowered down to all fours, muzzles extended, teeth bared, growling softly at one another.

I scuttle backwards into the corner as much as I can, my fear paralyzing me, making me unable to run. Would I run if I could? I'm not sure. I've never seen a wolf shifter in his wolf shape. I don't know what part of their brain is dominant. Is it the animal part or the human part? Do they remember me even? Do they know that they are here to protect me?

At that moment, Fynn turns his face to me. It's not his face anymore. But, they are his eyes. The eyes never change, even when the entire body does. His eyes are kind. I know he recognizes me. He knows why he is here. Anderson follows suit. They take two steps back, sheltering me with their hairy, lupine bodies. Somehow, my tension weakens. I am able to breathe properly again. The sight before me isn't fear-provoking any longer.

I look over at Sven and Kayne, and see that they also changed themselves into wolves. But, I can't take my eyes off of Fynn and Anderson. Their fur is glossy, thick, silvery white. Their paws scrape the cement floor we found ourselves on, and there is rage in their gazes. They are here for revenge. We all are.

They turn back at our enemies, their neck muscles protruding through the smooth fur. They are confident, bold. They feel no fear, if they ever did as humans. Suddenly, Fynn looks up at the ceiling, his wolfish silhouette on the wall opposite us extending. His howl fills the air around us. His hymn tells me everything will be alright. I need worry no more.

Without warning, Fynn lunges at one of the wolf figures opposite him. Anderson immediately does the same. What follows is a bloody dance of fangs and claws, torn fur and skin, digging teeth and howls.

A part of me wants to look away, but another part can't seem to take my eyes off of them. They are so majestic. Fearless. They are stripped of every bad aspect of being a human, and they are left with their lupine ferocity, but still with enough consciousness to know exactly what they are doing and what they're fighting for.

Fynn is fighting like there is no tomorrow. He takes blows and bites, but gives twice as many in return. Anderson is more cautious. He carefully deals his blows, he isn't taking as many. Just as in character, these two differ in their approach to fighting as well.

Their paws scrape against the cement floor as they jump and land on their feet, if not onto their enemies' bodies. Every bite into their bodies I feel like my own wound. We are interconnected, our souls intertwined, even though our bodies never united, not even once. I watch them, wondering how something like this could even happen to me.

Unexpectedly, Kayne plunges at Fynn, and manages to bring him down. Fynn growls, but Kayne has already dug his teeth into the soft flesh of Fynn's neck.

"No!" I scream, afraid that this attack might render Fynn motionless.

Led by some invisible force, feeling like I'm floating a few inches off the ground and my feet are not even touching it, I rush towards Fynn. Kayne has his back turned to me, his teeth still inside Fynn's neck, unwilling to let go.

My body seems to have a mind of its own, a mind that is unafraid to do even the scariest thing to save the ones she loves. I squeeze the little knife tightly in my hand, not even sure if it could hurt someone like Kayne. I have only one chance, and I need to make it count.

With the corner of my eye, I see that Anderson's got the upper hand on Sven, so he doesn't need help. But, he also can't help Fynn. I'm his only hope, unless Kayne release the grip on his neck, but that is probably not happening.

Neither Fynn nor Kayne notice me coming. That gives me the element of surprise, so I jump onto Kayne's back, one hand grabbing at his thick fur and the other driving the knife into the side of his neck. Before I extract it, I make sure to twist the knife upward, then forcefully pull it out. As I reach to stab him again, Kayne shakes me off of him, and I drop to the ground. Fynn is breathing heavily, and I wrap my arms around him, protecting him with my body.

But, Kayne is bleeding heavily. He can barely stand up. He teeters to the left, then to the right, then his front legs drop down.

"You.... bitch..." he manages to muster, before his body slumps down like a puppet whose strings got loose and there was no one to keep it going any longer.

I watch as the blood trickles out of his wound, and I know he's a goner. I've hit the artery, even though I had no idea where I was stabbing.

"Sometimes..." I hear Fynn try to say, "we have more luck than brains..."

He coughs immediately after, but he manages to get up. I check his neck. I need to remove his thick fur to see the bite marks.

"Does it hurt?" I ask.

"A little," he admits. "But, he didn't have the good luck you had."

I smile. His muzzle looks so weird. And the words that he's saying sound a little distorted, but I understand him.

At that moment, I remember Anderson, and I turn to him. Sven is lying on the ground. He looks unconscious. Anderson is breathing heavily, already having transformed back into his human form.

"Come on, grandpa," Anderson laughs, mocking Fynn. "Don't tell me that bastard almost got you?"

He walks over to Fynn, and rubs his hand through Fynn's fur, which is now slightly stained with blood.

"That's a nasty bite, but you'll live," he assures him. "Now, what am I going to wear in public?"

It's only then that I realize that Anderson is butt naked. Their transformation made them tear their clothes off their backs, so they had nothing to put on. Fynn slowly transforms back, and I try not to show how uneasy that crackling sound makes me. But, I can't hide it.

"You'll get used to it," Anderson smiles.

"Does it hurt?" I ask.

"Like a motherfucker," he chuckles. "That's why we only do it when it's necessary. Never just for fun or for show."

"You... did it for me?" I manage to whisper.

Fynn joins our intimate little circle, and I don't even mind that both of them are naked. It doesn't take away from the sanctity of the moment.

"We'd do anything for you," Fynn says this time. "Haven't you figured that out already?"

At the same time, we all spread our arms around one another, and we remain like that hugging, for a long time. Then, I suddenly remember.

"But... my father?" I take a step back, the first to break our hug. "We can't ask them now where he is."

All three of us look at the two dead bodies lying in front of us.

"Dead men tell no secrets," Anderson reminds us.

"How am I going to find out where my father is now?"

I am overcome with all the emotions, and I drop down to my knees, bursting out into tears. I'm sobbing uncontrollably, and Anderson is the first to wrap his arms around me. He doesn't say anything. He doesn't know what, and neither do I. I just know that I survived, but at the expense of my father's life. I wanted at least one more moment, just one, just to tell him that I don't think he is to blame for anything that's happened. We can't be held responsible for what other people do. We can only get entangled into it.

"Wait," Fynn suddenly says.

I know the sound of that voice. I know that tone. I've gotten to know him enough to recognize when he's on the verge of something, something important.

"What is it?" I stop crying, taking my hands off my face. Anderson also releases me from his embrace.

"Where was that house?" Fynn asks, looking like he got lost in his own thoughts, but he is trying to let us in.

"What house?" Anderson interferes.

"The one we burned down, with Kayne in it," Fynn reminds him. "Where was it?"

"Wait," Anderson taps his chin with the tips of his fingers in an effort to remember. "Wasn't it by the boondocks?"

"I can't remember. Are you sure?"

"Not a hundred percent, but it's as good a guess as any," Anderson shrugs. "Why?"

"Well, Kayne was obsessed with revenge, wasn't he?" He pauses, allowing us to nod quickly. "He did all of this because he wanted to get back at Hugo, and at us. So, there is only one logical place where he would leave him."

"You don't mean – "

"Yeah," Fynn nods gravely. "We need to get to that house. Now."

Chapter 24

"Are you sure my dad's there?" I ask, sitting on the backseat of the fast moving car.

Anderson is driving, and I can see the tight grip of his hands on the steering wheel. He wants to get us there as soon as possible, and I fear that every second counts. That is, if my father is even there, which is something we can't be sure of.

"That's my best guess," Fynn replies in his usual nothing-is-certain manner. "If he isn't there, then I really don't know where he could be. But, knowing Kayne, that's not only a possibility, but a probability."

I know this is as hopeful as his words would ever get, and I'm grateful for them. I huddle in the backseat, wishing for a blanket, but my body is still functioning under the strain of the adrenaline rush, and I don't even feel the chill of the night.

We drive in silence, each of us lost in their own thoughts, fighting our own demons. Somehow, I feel like there are less of mine. This nightmare is almost over. The persons who were responsible for this will never be brought to justice, but at least they will never do any harm again. That in itself is a solace of some sort.

As for my father, that lack of knowledge still bears heavily upon my soul. I look out the window, into the darkness, and wonder if that is what he sees if he is still alive. Is he breathing his last breath? Is he breathing at all?

All those questions are pressing onto my soul heavily. I feel like the burden of the world is on my back. I want to know. That's all I want. Even if the knowledge will bring me more pain, but anything is better than not knowing.

The drive is endless. We all shake and rattle on the dirt road that seems to take us into more darkness. A part of me wonders if this darkness will ever end, or will it just continue indefinitely?

Finally, the car stops. The bright lights are on, but I can't see anything in front of us. Just pure, unadulterated darkness that seems to mock our efforts at finding what we are looking for.

"We're here," Fynn informs us, even though it's unnecessary.

Still, no one gets out of the car. Not yet. My legs seem frozen. I'm petrified with the possibility that my father isn't here. Because, if we don't find him here, than he could be anywhere in the entire world, and he could be waiting for me to come and get him. The thought of him waiting somewhere, hurt and alone, brings tears to my eyes.

At that moment, Anderson turns to me. "Hey," his voice is soft and gentle, as always. Nothing changes it, and that constant returns some of my courage. "We'll find him."

"You can't promise that," I hear myself say, surprising everyone in the car.

"You also can't not promise," Fynn adds, and I chuckle against all conscious effort not to do so.

I sigh and without thinking, open the door and jump out. The guys immediately do the same. For a moment, we're in obscure darkness, the lights of the car gone. Fynn takes out a flashlight, and switches it on. It beams a long line of luminous path, like an angelic messenger. He aims it at something in the distance. I try to focus my eyes on it, but it's too far away. It's one of those things you see only if you know what you are looking for.

"There," Fynn points his index finger in the direction of the flashlight. "That's the house."

"Technically, it's not a house anymore," Anderson corrects.

He walks over to me. I hear his feet grinding the gravel. It feels soothing to know he's around, to know they're both around, and I don't have to go through this alone.

"Two of the outer walls are still standing tall," Anderson explains. "At least, they were the last time I was there."

"You went there?" Fynn asks.

"Just passing by," Anderson quickly replies, not wanting to elaborate more, and Fynn doesn't push him. "But everything else is grounded. There's nothing left."

"If there's nothing left, then why are we going there?" I suddenly interfere. "That doesn't make sense."

"You see, that house was special," Fynn explains, as we slowly start to walk over to the subject of our conversation. "It was used in the old days as a safe house for runaway slaves. Of course, that was a long time ago, but anyone who's ever been inside and knows what the house was used for, knows the outline of it. And, even though the upper, ground level is reduced to cinder, there is still an underground part. I think that's how Kayne managed to escape. We neglected to cover it, and, you know the rest."

"So, you think he was keeping my dad somewhere in the basement?" I wonder.

The crickets are loud, much louder than my thoughts, which are swarming inside of me like angry bees. I walk slowly, each step more insecure than the previous one. But, I still follow. There is no other path but this one.

"It's more of a whole underground level," Anderson takes over. "There is a big room underground, and tunnels that led away from the house. We thought that the tunnels were closed. There was an implosion of the ground at some point, and the tunnels were off limits. But, we didn't check it when... you know."

I can't see him clearly, but I know what he is doing. He is raking his fingers through his hair, nervously, trying to calm himself down.

"That's why we need to check the bottom level of the house," Fynn concludes.

"That sounds hopeful," I say it out loud, expecting that this will make it more believable.

"It's our only shot," Fynn adds.

"It's our best shot," Anderson chimes in as well.

I know they're on my side, and each of them, in his own special way, is trying to convince me to be strong and not to give up, no matter what we find there. Or, what we don't find.

It takes us a few more steps to the house. It is still as Anderson claimed it. Two walls still stand strong, perched together by a corner. They're just naked brick, with a single hole in them that once used to be a window. I'm guessing that it probably had a lovely view, one that whoever watched through, enjoyed. But now, all it shows is obscurity.

"Where is the cellar?" I look around, following Fynn's flashlight. "Will we be able to find it in the dark?"

"We can't wait until daytime," Fynn replies. "If he's here, and if he's wounded, he might not have hours to go."

That thought breaks me. But, I try to focus on the good and remain positive.

"There's too much rubble on the floor," Fynn snorts. "It's impossible to find a door that's kept hidden even in the daytime."

"Then try!" I hear myself shout, even though that's not what I intended.

The flashlight flickers for a moment, as if Fynn's hand trembled upon hearing me raise my voice.

"Sorry, I – "

But, I'm not allowed to finish. I feel Anderson's hand around my shoulders and his voice in my ear.

"It's fine," he soothes me. "Just let it out if you need to. We're here. We're not going anywhere."

My lips quiver, and I bite on my lower lip to calm down.

"This was the main room," I hear Fynn talk, and it sounds like he's talking to himself. "The entrance door was there." The flashlight points in the opposite direction. "The Southern window was there. And, the trap door was just through the fireplace."

I listen to his words, filled with hope. The flashlight tells his story, and I pray to God that he is right, that his memory serves him well. He runs over to one of the standing walls and gets down to his knees. I only notice the Moonlight at this point, and it seems like it's starting to burn brighter, as if the Moon itself wants us to find our path, it doesn't want us to stay lost.

I can see outlines of the men with me, Fynn's crouching body, as the flashlight points at the floor which he is so frantically trying to clear. I hear commotion, rubble being thrown to the side, the rolling of small pebbles and crackling of dried out branches.

"There!" Fynn shouts victoriously.

Anderson and I run over to help him.

"Help me with this!" Fynn instructs us, pointing the flashlight at a wooden door in the floor, which has something akin to a brass door knocker. I remember those from our old weekend house in the mountains, the one dad had to sell at some point, because it reminded him of mom too much. But, the door was the same.

Anderson grabs the door knocker, and Fynn tries the sides. They both grunt with exasperation, and it takes them three tries to finally open it. The door unfastens with a loud screeching sound, and a huge cloud of dust escapes it, making all of us cough.

"How do we get down?" I dare to look into the hold, but without Fynn's flashlight, I can't see anything.

"There should be a ladder or something," Anderson tells me.

The flashlight reveals exactly that. It looks old and worn out, unsafe to climb, but that won't stop me. I adjust myself to go inside, but Fynn grabs me by the elbow.

"Where do you think you're going?" he snarls. "Are you crazy? We don't know what or who's in there."

"My dad?"

"I'll go down, and if I need help, I'll call for Anderson," he orders me. "You stay here and don't move."

I open my mouth to object, but nothing comes out. Instead, I exhale loudly, and obey. My silly ideas have gotten us here. If I hadn't made him take a walk with me, they wouldn't have taken Anderson in the first place. Perhaps it's best just to do as I'm told this time.

Fynn goes down, and I huddle close to Anderson, as we remain in darkness.

"Are you scared?" he asks me.

"Only that my father might not be here."

"If he's not here, we'll look for him elsewhere. He has to be somewhere. And, we'll find him. I promise."

I lean over and rest my head on his shoulder. Without anticipating it, I feel his lips on my forehead as he plants a soft kiss on it. My heart flutters like a butterfly's wings, soft at first, then with a strength to move mountains.

"I need help over here!" Fynn suddenly shouts from inside.

Anderson immediately jumps into the hole, not even looking where exactly he's stepping. I hear a blaring thud noise as he drops to the ground, then the rushing of footsteps. The resonances of commotion reach me, but no matter how hard I peer into the darkness, I see nothing.

"Did you find him?" I shout into the hole, hearing my own echo.

Instead of a reply, the flashlight appears, shining through the hole, then upward in my direction.

"Can you lower yourself a little into the hole?" Fynn asks. "We need you to grab his hands, then pull as hard as you can!"

My mind goes blank. "You found him!?"

"Just pull him up!" Fynn repeats, and I immediately do as I'm told.

I reach into the hole, and the flashlight illuminates my father's slumbering face.

"Is he alright!?" I whimper, as I grab his arms, and start pulling up with all my might.

No one replies. We're all huffing, grunting, moaning, and trying to get my father out of the black hole he was in. It takes us a while, but finally we manage to do it.

I adjust my father's body onto the dirty floor, and immediately reach for his pulse. I can barely feel it, but it's still there.

"He's alive," I whisper, overwhelmed with joy and relief.

"He needs to go to the hospital," Fynn neglects what I said. "Now."

The flashlight points at his stomach. His shirt is stained with caked blood. There is so much of it.

"Let's get him to the car," Anderson urges us.

Fynn and Anderson manage to prop my father up on his feet, with his hands over each of their shoulders. We walk back to the car slowly, dragging my father's unconscious body, as I run around them, feeling like there is nothing I can do but burst out into tears. But, that would only make things worse.

We found him – that's what matters. Now, we need to focus on getting him to the hospital on time, and saving his life.

Chapter 25

The white lights of the hospital are too bright. My eyes hurt and my whole body is aching for a good night's rest, but I know that even if I lay down, I won't be able to fall asleep. Not while my father is lying in a hospital bed, with all those tubes sticking out of his body, tying him up to the machines.

"Want me to go get you another coffee?" I hear Anderson offer, as he gets up from his seat.

Fynn is sitting opposite us, his head buried in his hands. To some passer-by, it looks like he might be sleeping, but I know he's not.

"Their coffee's crap," I mumble. "But, yeah, I want one."

He smiles at me, squeezes my shoulder gently, and then walks away. The images of seeing my dad dragged out of that hole in the ground, barely alive, will haunt me for as long as I'm living. I know that. But, all I need is for him to stay with me, so I can build more memories, and so I can forgive him. So, I can forgive myself.

I get up and walk over to Fynn. He doesn't lift his gaze, even though he knows I'm sitting next to him.

"We found him," I tell him, as if it's news and he has no idea.

Only now does he look up at me. "But, look at the condition we found him in."

"My dad is a tough guy," I smile, trying to convince us both of this. "He'll make it."

"We were supposed to make sure this didn't happen," Fynn tells me.

"Listen to me now," I suddenly take his hands into mine forcefully, like I'm taking back something that was always mine, but he only held it for a little while. "This isn't your fault. It's not. You did exactly what you were supposed to do and exactly how you were supposed to do it. It's only thanks to you and Anderson that I'm alive, that my dad is finally safe in a hospital, and he can start healing."

He doesn't say anything to that. He only shakes his head. I know he doesn't believe me.

"I didn't do my job. I failed you again. I failed all of you."

"That's not true," I assure him. "You can't be held responsible for everything someone else does. It's not your responsibility to predict the actions of others."

"But, it is to try and counteract them. That's my job as a cop."

"And, you did exactly that!"

"You saved me. It wasn't the other way around," he looks down, as if he's ashamed of this.

His reaction makes me sad. Not because I wanted him to be all grateful, but I simply wanted him to appreciate what I had done. I wanted him to realize how much it took of myself to do that. However, he doesn't feel anything apart from remorse.

"I'm sorry you see it that way," I whisper. "In the end, does it really matter who saves who, if the good guys win?"

I don't wait for him to reply. Instead, I get up and see Anderson walking over with three cups of that poor excuse of a coffee in his hands.

"Here you guys go," he smiles. "A fresh batch of bat piss for everyone."

I chuckle, and look at him gratefully.

"What happened here?"

He glances over at Fynn, but before I can tell him anything a nurse walks over to us.

"Miss Holloway?" She smiles at me cordially, bringing some more of that painful whiteness with her.

She has a slick ponytail, and a very minimum amount of makeup. Still, she looks refreshed. Definitely not like someone who works in a hospital, and who we just caught on night shift.

"Yes?" I turn to face her, my heart trembling with fear at what she is about to tell me.

"Your father has been taken care of," she starts slowly, accentuating every word, like it's something she has rehearsed for a play. In a way, she has. "He is in the special care unit on the third floor – "

"Can I see him?" I interrupt her, but she remains calm and polite.

"I'm afraid that's impossible tonight. The doctor needed to put him into an induced coma. This was necessary for the purposes of reaching a level of sedation that is referred to as burst suppression."

She keeps talking like a teacher explaining a tough math problem to her students for the third time in a row. Still with a soft smile on her face and still with the same level of patience.

"There has been significant swelling in the brain, which results in painful pressure and damage of the brain tissue. Your father's brain needs to rest, so that his entire body may recover and so that his brain swelling reduces. His brain is fully sedated for a few seconds, then it forces itself into a few seconds of activity bursts. His brain is kept active, but at the same time, these periods of rest are crucial for his healing process."

"When will he wake up?"

"That depends on the speed of his recovery," she explains. "We can't give any estimates. It can be anywhere from a few days to a few months. Sometimes, it's even years."

"Years?"

"Yes, I'm sorry," she speaks, pressing her thin lips together, expressing regret.

"Can I just see him? I won't talk to him. Just through the glass," I plead.

The nurse's lips part, probably in an effort to find a polite way to refuse my request, but she sees the tears in my eyes. She hears the pain in my voice.

"Just through the window," she finally agrees. "And, just for a few seconds."

"Of course," I nod quickly. "Will you guys wait for me here?"

Fynn and Anderson nod, as I wave a little awkwardly, allowing the nurse to lead me to the third floor. While riding the elevator, she turns to me.

"You're lucky. You brought him in just in time."

Those words hit me like a ton of bricks. I was this close to losing him. I'm still close, but I won't let go. I'll hold on til the very last breath in my body.

"Also, I haven't mentioned it, but I shall need to report this to the police. Gunshot wounds are always reported."

"Those two men with me are police officers," I explain, as the door pings and opens up for us, letting us out.

"Then, they can sort it out with the officer on duty," she nods.

"Of course," I smile. "We have nothing to hide."

She looks at me, as if she's trying to find out if I'm lying or not. Her gaze is long and steady. I wonder how many patients she saw dying. Did she see something in their eyes? Did she see the window to their soul?

She turns away without another word, and leads me to the room at the end of a quiet, and much less busy hallway. She stops in front of a small, rectangular window.

"This is your father's room."

She steps a little to the side, so I can take a look inside. As I do so, I gasp silently. His head is wrapped up. There is a tube coming out of his mouth. An IV is connected to his right arm. The machines in the room, next to his bed, are beeping steadily. I press my hand to my lips.

I remember getting my appendix out when I was a girl. I was petrified of the operation, and even more so because they said that neither of my parents could spend the night at the hospital. They could be there all day, but at night, they'd needed to let me rest. My mom promised me all the ice cream I could eat once I got out. And, she made good on that promise. But, dad didn't say anything. He just stared at me in my hospital pajamas and at the place where the wound was, underneath the covers. He didn't speak much, but he hugged me and kissed me much more than usual. I never thought much of it before. But, now, it all makes sense.

Seeing your loved one in this situation brings out something in you, something primal, some primordial fear about the fleetingness of life, and the fact that it takes one single second to erase us from the chronicles of this life. It's that easy. And, while you're walking the streets out in the world, this knowledge is in the back of your mind. You barely pay any attention to it. But, when you're at the hospital, the constant reminders are there, right in front of you, and no matter how hard you want to close your eyes, they don't go away.

"Will he be OK?" I ask, sounding like it's not a question for her, but for the Universe. Only this time, the nurse speaks for it.

"He has everything going for him," she replies vaguely, but her smile soothes me.

"Thank you," I take her by the hand.

I quickly let go, realizing how unprofessional that must be, but my gratitude is immense and a mere thank you in words wouldn't be enough.

"Can I come tomorrow?" I ask her.

"It's best if you rest," she advises me. "I don't know what's happened, but you all look like you've been through Hell and back. Just go home and try to get some rest. We have your contact info, and if there is any change, we shall notify you immediately."

The last thing I want to do right now is leave my father again. But, I know there is no point in me staying here at the hospital, just waiting. I need to rest. My body has become numb, but once the sensations come back to me, I'll probably be in a world of pain.

"You're right," I nod. "That's what I'll do."

"You can find your own way back?"

"Of course," I smile. "And, thank you again."

I turn and walk down the hallway, towards the elevator. I press the button, allowing the exhaustion to take over. Not even those crappy hospital coffees are helping any longer. What I need is a nice, long shower and my own bed.

I wonder if I can sleep in my bed now. Is the nightmare finally over? Am I finally safe?

I reach the lower floors, and see Fynn and Anderson still there. Their presence doesn't surprise me. I walk over to them, with a smile on my face.

"How bad is it?" Anderson is the first to ask.

"Pretty bad," I nod. "He looks like a hospital puppet."

"He'll be fine," Anderson smiles. "If I know Hugo, and I do... trust me."

Fynn walks over to us. He looks embarrassed. It's the look he had when Anderson told him that he was behaving like an asshole, and Fynn knew Anderson was right.

"Listen – " he starts, but I won't let him.

"No."

I shake my head. I take him by the hand, and I take Anderson's hand with my other.

"This isn't the time for more explanations or apologies or anything like that. I just need you guys to take me home. My home. Can you do that for me?"

Anderson looks over at Fynn, then back at me.

"Girl, I thought you'd never ask."

Chapter 26

We drive back home, and I unlock the door. The familiar smell hits my nostrils. It smells like home. It smells like the carpet mom bought when she and dad went to Turkey on their honeymoon. It smells like the old leather chair that dad never wanted to get rid of because it belonged to some important finance guy dad always looked up to, and then found that chair on some charity auction, then paid a ton of money for it, even though it wasn't worth even half of that. It smells like our bookshelf, like the potted plants on the window sill, still surviving and blossoming, despite everything.

"Everything OK?" Anderson asks, seeing that I just opened the door, but I'm not going in.

"Everything is fine," I smile.

I take a step in, but Fynn grabs me by the elbow.

"Let me guess," I frown, jokingly. "You need to check to make sure it's safe."

"See?" Fynn elbows Anderson gently in the stomach. "I don't even need to say it anymore. She knows everything."

We all chuckle, feeling like a huge cloud just got lifted from above us. Fynn and Anderson go in first, instructing me to remain downstairs. It takes them a while to check every room, but when they're finally done, they return with a victorious smile on their faces.

"Milady," Anderson bows, "thy mansion is clean."

"Wonderful!" I jump from the little sofa I almost fell asleep in, and start clapping.

"Now, we need to head back to the – " Anderson continues.

"You aren't leaving me alone, are you?" I whine.

"Well," Anderson looks at Fynn. "We could stay, for the night. Sleep on the sofa or the floor."

"There are plenty of guest rooms, don't be silly," I tell him.

"We could just call in tonight and sort everything out tomorrow, at the station," Anderson looks over at Fynn. "What do you say?"

Fynn sighs heavily, more heavily than in the last few weeks.

"I think that's the best idea I've ever heard."

"Well, alright then," Anderson grins. "We got a sleepover on our hands. I'll quickly ring the station, and then..."

"Shower and bed," Fynn smirks. "For everyone."

"Oh, I doubt I could sleep after all this commotion," I chuckle. "Plus, I fell asleep on the sofa, while you guys were checking the place out. I think I had my power nap."

"What?" Anderson starts laughing. "You better not try to keep us awake all night long with your girl talk and shit."

I laugh at his comment, even though that definitely doesn't sound like a bad idea.

"I promise, if I can't sleep, I'll just watch a movie or something."

But, there is something that won't let me be. I stop, and turn to them again. Their eyes are inquisitive. They know there are still some questions left unanswered.

"What is it?" Fynn asks. "You look troubled."

"There is something that's still bugging me."

"Tell us," Anderson urges.

"Kayne mentioned something in my dad's safe," I hesitate. "What is it?"

Fynn looks over at Anderson, then back at me again.

"Your dad had Kayne's dental records," Fynn explains. "I have no idea how he got a hold of them. But, he was always afraid that we didn't finish the job. As it turned out, we really hadn't. So, he kept that record safe, knowing he might need it at some point, if his worst suspicions came true. Unfortunately, none of us expected the Chief to be... Kayne."

Fynn's admission left me confused, but relieved at the same time. So, it wasn't money or something that might again come back to haunt us. Kayne was dead. For real this time. And, his dental records bore no relevance any longer.

"It's really over, isn't it?" I sigh, even managing to smile.

"It really is," Fynn assures me.

I nod, walking out of the room slowly, my shoulders much less tense than before. After about half an hour, we all meet back in the lounge, all of us having taken our showers and having ordered a pizza, which arrived only a few minutes before. I'm wearing my pajamas, not sexy at all, but comfortable. I guess that's always been me.

The guys helped themselves to some plain t-shirts from my dad's closet, and some sweatpants. I'm surprised my dad still has some of those in his closet, always preferring to dress to the nines, but I suppose that's also one of those things left from the time of my mother. She liked things easy and spontaneous, and with her around, that was always so easy. After she was gone, both me and dad found it difficult to be spontaneous. It was simply too hurtful. So, planning ahead became comforting. Planning what to do, where to go, even what to wear. The heart is pacified by the strangest things, it seems.

Returning with the pizza from the kitchen, Anderson places it on the small coffee table, and then rests a Coke six pack next to it.

"Look what I found in the pantry," he beams proudly.

"Pizza just isn't pizza without Coke," I smile. "Well done."

As soon as I take the first bite, I realize how ravenous I am. I also realize that I can't remember when was the last time I had something to eat, and neither can the guys. We wolf down the whole thing within minutes, the guys so relaxed that Anderson even burps loudly a few times, which provides him with a frown from Fynn and a chuckle from me.

"Maddie, there is something I'd like to tell you," Fynn suddenly starts, sitting next to me on the sofa.

Anderson is quiet, resting on the armchair, a little further away from us.

"You interrupted me at the hospital, but I think the right time is as good as any."

"What is it?" I smile.

"I can be a real hardass," he nods.

"Boy, don't we know it!" Anderson interrupts, and we all laugh.

I don't remember the last time it felt this good to laugh, and I welcome the sensation.

"But, all I did and said was so I could keep you safe."

"I know that."

"So, I'd like to apologize."

"Apologize?" I look over at Anderson, not believing this is happening. "You?"

"Yes," he nods. "I was harsh at times when it was uncalled for. And, I apologize."

"Oh, it's all water under the bridge," I smile. "Don't worry about it."

"See?" Anderson beams. "I told you. She's amazing."

"Wow," I exclaim, my head cocking to one side. "I never thought I'd hear that from either of you."

"I never doubted that actually," Fynn adds, in his characteristic way.

"Oh, my God, was that just a compliment from the both of you?" I smirk.

"I think so, yeah," Anderson nods. "What do you say, Fynn?"

"Absolutely."

I feel myself blushing with all this attention, and at the same time, I realize how welcome it is. In the beginning of this nightmare, I could sense that there was something between us, between me and Anderson, between me and Fynn, despite his hardass behavior – to use his words.

Suddenly, I feel Fynn's hand cover mine, gently, gentler than I ever thought his touch could be. Anderson gets up, and sits on the other side of the couch.

"You're the perfect woman, Madeleine," he whispers right into my ear, and I don't know why the use of my full name coming out of his mouth arouses me to such an extent.

But, I love it. Every hair on my body is on its end. My skin is electrified by Fynn's touch. My ears pricked up to the sound of Anderson's honey-sweet voice.

Fynn's fingers intertwine with mine, and Anderson removes my hair from my neck. Softly, one kiss lands on my skin. Then, another. And, another.

"All we want to do is make you feel amazing, even more amazing than you are," Anderson murmurs.

I sigh deeply, closing my eyes. I can't believe this is really happening. I want it. I've wanted it from the first moment I saw them, but I was too scared to realize it. Now, with all that danger out of our way, I can finally let go.

I feel my heart thumping wildly in my chest. Fynn leans in softly, and presses his lips to mine. A fire burns somewhere deep inside of me. Our kiss is passionate, but still gentle and soft. Our tongues intertwine, as Anderson keeps planting even softer, butterfly kisses on my neck and shoulder.

"This is what we've been thinking about from the first moment we saw you," Anderson whispers, and exhilaration flares inside of me.

A tidal wave of heat rushes down my spine, then back up. I feel myself getting wet, and they've barely touched me. I'm throbbing somewhere deep inside. The teasing has lasted too long already. I'm eager. The desire builds up in me.

"Me, too," I whisper back feeling emboldened, when Fynn's lips pull away.

I moan softly, biting my lower lip.

"Is that all you've been thinking about?" Anderson bites my earlobe, and a million little goosebumps rush up my body. "Feeling us inside of you?"

"Yes..." I moan again.

"Soon?" he asks, his fingers stroking my bare arms.

"Now," I whisper.

"We in a hurry?"

He blows hot air onto my neck, raising all my hairs on their end. Suddenly, he gets up, and offers Fynn and me his hands. Together, we walk back to my bedroom, and as we're standing in the middle of the room, my oversized t-shirt just slides down onto the floor. I'm left in only my panties.

"God, you're perfect," Anderson mutters, standing behind me.

His hands travel slowly over my body, feeling every indentation, every hill, every protruding bone with the tips of his fingers. I help Fynn get out of his clothes, with Anderson's hands still on my body. Then, I turn to him, and do the same.

They take me to the bed, and I lay down onto my back. The thin fabric of my panties feels suffocating somehow. But, I dare not take it off. There is thunder in my groin, in my chest, in my heart.

Fynn's lips clash with mine again, more demanding this time. As we're kissing, I feel Anderson's fingers sliding my panties down my legs, spreading them forcefully. I moan into Fynn's mouth, noiselessly.

The heat of Anderson's breath hits my velvet underground like an implosion. My back arches, as his tongue introduces itself to my soft, needy folds. I gasp with desire. My toes curl, as Anderson keeps licking my pussy. I adjust myself a little closer to him, all the while cupping Fynn's face with the palms of my hands, as if scared of letting him go.

Pleasure shudders through my entire body, as Anderson's lips pull at my clit, sucking it. My whole body starts to tremble, surrendering to the sensation that threatens to swallow me whole. He is so good, it's as if he knows my body better than I know it myself. I'm his instrument, and he is playing the sweetest music I've ever heard. His fingers join in the fun, sliding in only one at first.

Fynn's hands are on my tits, my nipples hard and erect, begging for more. There is a soundless hum in my mind, sheer bliss. My legs hook over Anderson's shoulders, his tongue working with his fingers deeper, harder, picking up the rhythm.

I'm about to explode. Implode. Dissolve into a million little pieces. As if sensing this, Anderson quickly pulls away, leaving a vast emptiness where his tongue and face once were.

"Ahhh..." I moan, my body begging him to come back, not to leave me like this.

Fynn pulls away, and instead of his lips, I find his erect cock, ready to be worshipped. My mouth opens obediently, taking in only the tip at first. At the same time, Anderson returns with his devil tongue, making it all even more intense.

I play with Fynn's cock, my lips curling around it, sucking, licking, as Anderson finds fury in friction, leading me closer and closer to the brink. He is focused on my clit now, rubbing the perfect spot, his fingers sliding inside of me, making it increasingly difficult to breath.

"Oh, my God..." I shout, slurping my own saliva from Fynn's throbbing cock.

My orgasm hits me fast, an elated wave of pleasure that cuts me in half. Fynn's cock flops out of my mouth, allowing me to fully partake in this moment. The rapture is too much. My body tenses, convulses, as Anderson's tongue continues relentlessly, burying my pussy in more licks and finger fucks.

Slowly, I float down to earth, light as a cloud. My eyes are closed. I feel like I'm made of cotton candy and rainclouds. But, they don't let me rest.

"Do you have a condom?" Anderson asks.

I get up, open the bedside drawer, and get one out from all the way in the back. It's actually from the time my best friend gave it to me with the instructions to have fun. I remember just shoving it in there. Well, now, I'm having fun.

We get back onto the bed, and I give it to him. He rips the condom wrapper and rolls it on. My legs are spread out once more, and I feel the tip of Anderson's cock press against my still leaking pussy. He slides in effortlessly, filling me up to the brim. He takes me in one long thrust.

"That feels so good..." I moan.

My eyelids lift in a haze, and Fynn is there again, his cock swollen and needy. His fingers claw my hair, pulling me closer onto him, making me take all of him in my mouth. Adrenalin surges through me. I crave them both so much. They set me on fire, I feel like I'm going to disintegrate, only to be reborn, like a Phoenix, from the ashes of my own death.

Fynn thrusts into my mouth, as Anderson fucks me. We all get carried away. Full satisfaction guaranteed with every single stroke. None of us is taking it slow. We're past that. Our tempo is united, rhythmical. It's a give and take of heavenly and hellish, pain and pleasure. We're bound and intertwined all three of us: mind, body and soul.

I suck Fynn off, using my tongue, my warm breath powerful, bringing him to the brink. My screams are born and they die inside of me. Our pleasure intensifies. Rising higher and higher, until we are no longer three different individuals. We are one.

I feel Fynn's cock rigid inside my mouth. Anderson thrusts harder and harder. There is an animal inside all of us, waiting, clawing to be released. Their effort is desperate.

My pussy and mouth clench together at the same time. We all go tumbling over the invisible edge, right into the abyss of ecstasy. Another orgasm, even more violent, more devastating than the previous one, scorches right through me. Anderson comes within seconds. He finishes inside of me, the condom keeping us all safe from any possible accidents. Fynn instantly roars, and fills my throat with his hot seed.

I feel two cocks pulsating inside of me, electrifying my every muscle. It's a storm of our own creation, and it takes us a while to come down to earth. The aftermath is indulgent. The sizzle is gone at this point, but it is easy to just enjoy the moment.

Our breathing returns to normal shortly. Fynn lies down next to me, my head on his shoulder. Anderson lies on his other side, his hand lying over Fynn's chest and my hips. Fynn turns and kisses the tip of nose. I lift my gaze, and for the first time ever, I see something I've never seen in his eyes before. There is vulnerability there. There is trust. There is love.

"I've never felt this way before," I hear him say.

"This is it for us," Anderson adds. "There is no going back now."

They give me a second, and I can't even think straight. I'm overjoyed.

"You don't have to decide right now," Fynn suddenly says more gravely. "I know this must be a lot to take in. Just know that we're not going anywhere. We'll be here, waiting for your decision. Then, we will do exactly as you instruct us. If you agree, we will stay by your side til the end. But, if you don't want that, all it takes is a single word, and we will disappear. You will never see us again."

"No," I grab at his chest, exactly where his heart is. "I don't want that. I mean, I want this. I want you. Both of you. I want us all to be together, and have babies, and live in the mountains, and share everything. The good, the bad, everything."

Neither of them says anything to that. I close my eyes. I don't need to see to know that we are all smiling. We are all happy. Finally, our real lives can begin.

Chapter 27

Anderson

When I wake up, the sunlight from the window tells me it's much later than it should be. I overslept. As usual. I turn to the other side of the bed, expecting either Fynn or Maddie, but neither of them is here. The sheets are cold. So, they must have been up for a while now.

I prop myself onto my elbows, looking around the room. I'm in Maddie's room. There are still some leftovers from her teenage days. Still some glittery shit on the big mirror. The jewelry that seems to belong to someone older and more sophisticated. Maybe her mom. And, a photo of the three of them, the whole family, in a small picture frame by that same mirror.

I remember Hugo back in the day. Ambitious. Cocky. I guess, we're all cocky and think we got the world by the balls when we know someone loves us. And, his wife loved him. That much was obvious to everyone. That was how Kayne knew he'd get him. Hugo cared about the money, but he was one of those people who always thought "Fuck it, I can just go make some more." But, he could never make another wife. Not like that one. And, Kayne knew it.

I get up, my cock exhausted from the sex last night, and grab the photo frame. Maddie looks so much like her mother. That's probably why Kayne targeted her for his final revenge blow.

I sigh, putting it back in its place, carefully. Hopefully, this shit storm is over now and we can go on with our lives. But, how? Will she agree to the more than unconventional life we would offer her? Or would she just say, no thanks?

I doubt that, after meeting her, we'd be able to find anyone like her. No way. She's one of a kind.

With those thoughts in mind, I find my t-shirt on the floor and a pair of sweatpants, and put them on. I walk downstairs, and hear chuckling in the kitchen.

"But, how can it be alive and dead at the same time?" Maddie asks, just as I'm walking into the kitchen.

They're both seated at the table, with a cup of coffee in their hands. She looks absolutely stunning. She is wearing just an oversized t-shirt. Her hair is in a messy bun, and she has that morning glow about her.

"So, who's alive and dead at the same time?" I wonder. "And, can that zombie make me a coffee, too?"

Maddie chuckles. "Sit down, I'll get you some coffee."

I do as she instructs, and Fynn smiles at me.

"Fynn was just telling me about the Schrödinger's cat," she explains.

"Not the cat again," I roll my eyes. "He's told me about it like five times already, and I still don't get it."

"You've never really been an intellectual, Anderson," Fynn mocks, good-humoredly.

"And, I'm doing just fine, thank you very much," I grin. "But, maybe Maddie can explain it to a layman better."

"Oh, I wish," she smiles, pouring me a fresh cup of heavenly coffee. "It just seems like a case of two parallel realities, you know, the cat is both alive and it's not alive. I mean, you can't know. The box is closed. So, both theories are in fact true, because neither can be disproved. At least, until there is an observation and reality kicks in."

"See!" Fynn nods enthusiastically. "That's exactly it. She gets it from the start."

"Well done," I give her a little clap, and we all laugh.

She brings her cup to her lips, and gazes at us from behind it, her eyes curious and wide.

"So, what's our plan for the day?" she suddenly wonders.

"Plan?" Fynn repeats.

"I know you guys need to go to the station, fill out a report, explain everything that's happened with Kayne," she nods.

"Absolutely," I nod. "I'll leave Fynn to handle that."

"So, what else is new?" Fynn snorts.

"I was thinking, maybe later we could hang out... or something," she adds, her cheeks blushing furiously.

"About that, Maddie – " Fynn starts.

"I don't mean to pressure you guys into anything," she suddenly shakes her head, as if she's said something wrong. "I probably shouldn't have pushed. Sorry."

"Whoa, whoa," I chuckle. "Hold your horses, girl. There's something we'd like to talk to you about."

"About what?" she asks.

"Fynn?" I look over at him. "You're better at this official stuff. Why don't you explain it to her?"

"Guys, you're really making me nervous here," she smiles, a little anxiously, as she waits for us to clarify.

"You always leave me with the difficult part of the job," Fynn grins. "Alright then."

He clears his throat a little, before continuing.

"The circumstances under which the three of us met were anything but ordinary. And, I think we all felt the same in the beginning. We were pushing you away, because it was too dangerous. I had no idea how this would end. And, I didn't even want to think about the worst possibility, which by the way, almost happened."

"Why don't you cut to the chase?" I poke fun at him, knowing he hates that.

"Then, why don't you do it, smart ass?" he grins back. "Anyway, Maddie... you know our story. Well, most of it. You know what we are. You know what we do. What you may not know is that everyone in our clan chooses their mate. The person we choose has to be special, in more ways than one. She has to fulfill many conditions, and I don't think I need to tell you that it's difficult finding the right partner, or in our case, a mate."

I watch her as she listens to him patiently. That lingering smile never leaves her face, and I'm sure that hers is the face I want to see for the rest of my life.

"A long time ago, Anderson and I vowed that we'd choose our mate together. That, as you can expect, makes things even more difficult, because not many would consider our offer. You... did. I can't even begin to tell you how surprised I was at that. I mean, I hoped. Anderson hoped, too. But, you just blew our minds. You are so amazing, Maddie."

She blushes at his words, and I want to wrap my arms around her, but I refrain from doing so. Fynn needs to tell her what we want, what we need from her, and we can only hope that she will agree.

"Maybe you already know what I want to tell you, what we both want to tell you."

He pauses, her smile widens a little. I can see it in her eyes that she knows. She senses. And, she likes it.

"Will you be our mate?" Fynn asks simply.

She looks at him, then at me.

"Will I be your only mate?" she suddenly asks, like a little child, afraid that she will have to share her favorite toy.

"Of course," Fynn actually laughs at this one, and I join in.

"I mean, you won't replace me with someone later on?" she blushes ever more as she asks this.

"We have only one mate," Fynn explains. "Til death do us part, as you like to vow to each other."

"I think I'd like that," she whispers.

I jump to her and wrap my arms around her thin little neck, as she is still seated on the chair. Fynn walks over to us slowly. He uses both hands to enshroud us both.

"So, is there anything I need to know about this?" she asks again, curiously.

"Like what?" I reply with another question, sitting back at the table.

"Like, will we all be living together?"

"Of course," Fynn nods. "No question about it."

"And, our kids – "

"Are our kids," he answers that one, too. "It doesn't matter whose sperm made it to the egg first."

He says it so seriously that we can't stop laughing at some point. Even he joins in. After a few moments of incessant laughter, she continues dreamily.

"And, where will we live?"

"I have a big house on the outskirts, just at the foot of a nearby mountain. I always wanted to live there once I settle down. And, I think Fynn agrees, as well."

"There's a view of the mountain from the window?" she smiles.

"It's breath-taking," I assure her. "And, you don't need to worry about anything. We'll take care of everything, of you, the kids, absolutely everything."

"Oh, I have no concerns about that," she beams. "You've proven yourselves to me more than once. I trust you with my life."

I feel as if someone grabbed my heart and won't let go. Maybe that's what love feels like. It's a bit scary. A bit overwhelming. But, you don't want that hand to ever let go of you, even if it does occasionally squeeze a little too tight.

Chapter 28

It's been a week since life has returned to usual. At least, it's trying to, and we are doing our best to accommodate the new developments. For the time being, while my dad is at the hospital, all three of us are still living in his mansion. I've taken it upon myself to keep up with the cleaning and the usual housework, with a little bit of hired help. After all, it's an unnecessarily huge house. I kept telling him to sell it, and just get a smaller one, maybe somewhere in the mountains, but his reasoning was always that he lived in this house with my mother, and he will die in it, too. I guess I understand.

I always thought living with someone would be difficult. After all, it's two souls adapting to a new level of existence: co-existence. And, with us, there are three souls. However, it's been nothing but smooth sailing. Anderson and Fynn are still very much different, but it is so easy to talk to them. I guess, it's easy to find common ground when all parties involved wish everyone to be happy. And, that's all I want, to be happy with the two of them.

It's lunch time, and only Anderson is home. Fynn is at the station. He is needed on some top secret president-related matter, and it's only him, so Anderson is given the day off. I thought he'd be a little offended, but he actually welcomed the day off, and spending it at home with me.

We sit down to have lunch together, and I relish his smile and his compliments about my new-found cooking skills.

"You always seem to outdo yourself with your meals," he smiles at me. "This meat is so tender and I love the sauce. Is that avocado?"

"Yes, and just FYI, you love me, so you have to say that," I giggle, waving a fork defensively in the air. "Don't think for a second that I don't know your game."

"No, I love you, so I don't have to say that, because you already love me and I don't need to butter you up. You're ours." He winks at me, then blows me a kiss.

"That's true," I shake my head jokingly at him. "But, - "

At that moment, the phone rings. I usually don't pick it up when I'm having a meal with them, but this time, a gut feeling tells me I need to.

"Sorry," I tell him, wiping my lips on the napkin, and then grabbing the phone.

"Yes?" I reply, without recognizing the caller number. "Yes, this is she... He is!? Oh, my God... yes... of course... Of course... I'll be right there, thank you. Goodbye."

I hang up the phone with trembling hands. My lips are dry, and I feel like I'm both out of breath and out of words to explain what just happened.

"What is it, Maddie?"

He gets up from the kitchen table and walks over to me. His hands rest on my shoulders, and I'm grateful for the support. Otherwise, I'm afraid I might slump down onto the floor, like a heavy bag of potatoes.

"My dad..." I manage to mutter. "He's awake."

"What are we waiting for?" he smiles widely. "Let's head to the hospital now."

"Just... need to grab my bag..."

I feel lost, like this isn't happening, like it's all some dream and I'm afraid I'll wake up, and we'll still be stuck in that old house, tied up to the chairs. But, Anderson's presence reminds me this is real. His hands in mine prove this is reality. And, I'll never have to be afraid again.

We reach the hospital quickly, and that same nurse welcomes us. She is wearing the same white outfit, only now it isn't as painful as that first time. Her hair is in a bun this time, and she is wearing more mascara than usual. It seems that even she looks like there is something to celebrate.

"Miss Holloway," she smiles at me, "I'm happy to tell you that your father is awake, and all of his vital signs are steady."

"That's wonderful..." I can barely speak from the tears that want to surge out.

This has been the moment I've been waiting for, and it is finally here. A tidal wave of relief washes over me, and I just let this realization sink in.

"We wanted to call you immediately. Now, you can see him, but only for a little while. We don't want to overstimulate him as that might not be beneficial to his recovery," she nods as she speaks, and I can only agree with that.

"Of course," I assure her. "I'll be very careful. Can I go in now?"

"Yes," she opens the door to his room, and I walk inside.

He is lying on the same bed, and it looks like an equal number of tubes is still connected to his body. His chest rises and lowers slowly, rhythmically. The beeping sounds of the machines fills up the room, so it's never completely quiet. I wonder how he will sleep now. He always prefers it full dark and completely silent, to rest properly.

I take a few steps towards his bed, and the sound of my footsteps makes him open his eyes. I hasten my steps and sit on a chair near the bed. I cup his hand with mine, careful with the IV insert. It looks shriveled, almost like it doesn't belong to him anymore, but to some much older man.

"Dad..." I whisper, overcome by emotion.

I'm not even trying to prevent my tears from streaming down my face. I just let them. But, the smile on my face is unbeatable. I have him back. Finally, I can say what he needs to hear, so that we can both move on.

"M..." he tries, but can't finish.

"Shhh," I gesture at him with my fingers not to try and speak. "You're too weak. Don't try to talk. Just listen, OK?"

I snivel a little, and he gives me a weak nod. I caress his stubby face. He's lost so much weight. He looks ill. Just looking at him makes me want to cry even more.

"You need a good shave, dad," I try a chuckle, and it works. I need to stay positive, for him and for myself. "We'll get you sorted out when you get home. Just focus on getting better and don't worry about anything else, OK? That's your number one priority now."

I keep nodding, like a stupid bobble head, but I don't know what else to do. This is hard. Harder than I thought. I see the pain in his eyes, and it's killing me.

"Dad... I'm so sorry about everything..." I start, not really knowing what words to use.

Not like I practiced it in front of the mirror. You can never practice this kind of a speech. Forgiveness comes from the heart, not from some rehearsed set of words. That's what my mother always taught me. Just to speak from my heart and let it be my guide. The mind might need some help occasionally in choosing the right words, but the heart always knows. It feels what needs to be said, so it's easy.

"I know what happened to mom, and I know you've been living with the guilt all these years..."

My voice trails away as I speak. I wipe the tears from my eyes. He doesn't say anything, but his eyes tell me that he knows.

"And... I haven't made it easy on you," I continue. "I want to tell you that I forgive you. I know that Mom forgives you, too. And most importantly, you should forgive yourself."

One stray tear rolls down his face, and I wipe it with my hand.

"Don't cry," I tell him. "Everything will be alright. Just come home, OK?"

He nods, more forcefully this time, like he wanted to convince me that he means it this time. I press my lips on his hand, softly. He is cold.

I adjust his blanket a little, and he gifts me a smile. I kiss his sweaty forehead, then squeeze his hand.

"I gotta go now, dad. But, I promise I'll be back soon, OK?"

It's getting harder and harder to talk, my words are swallowed by the tears that just won't stop.

"Later, alligator," I wave at him, then exit the room slowly.

Anderson is there, and he immediately wraps me up in a hug. I bury my nose into his neck, and we remain like that for a few moments. I feel like the whole world has stopped spinning, just for me, just so I could have this special moment, and I've never been more grateful for anything I had in my life.

"How is he?" Anderson asks, once I let go.

"Weak." My answer is honest. I guess, I picked up more from Fynn than I intended to. "But, he'll be fine. Us Holloways are like that. Resilient. You can't kill us."

Anderson chuckles, presses his lips to my temple, and we walk out of the hospital, hugging. I feel the newfound lightness in my step, and I know that life will be perfect from now on, because I will make sure that it is.

Chapter 29

That same evening, I'm sitting on the sofa, reading my book. Huddled underneath a small blanket, I can't really focus on what the heroine should do, and I can't really root for her, mostly because I can't stop smiling. I can't stop thinking how fortunate I am, to have everything I ever wanted, right by my side.

A little later, Anderson walks in. He has a mischievous smile on his face. His eyes are beaming.

"Come on," he says chirpily, without any introduction or explanation why, and offers me his hand.

"Where?" I smile, closing my book and taking him by the hand.

"You'll see," he tells me playfully. "Just be patient."

"You know that's not one of my strong suits," I laugh.

He takes me over to the ground floor bathroom, the one with the big bath tub. The upper floor bathrooms all have shower stalls instead.

"Now, close your eyes," he instructs me, before opening the door.

"OK," I reply, feeling giddy.

I hear him open the door, and he leads me in, my eyes still closed.

"Open."

The moment I open my eyes, I find an amazing oasis of relaxation inside. There are red and white candles scattered about the bathroom. There is a soft scent of jasmine permeating the air. I see my favorite bathing products in the corner of the bathtub, next to a glass of wine, filled to the brim.

"Wow," I gasp in awe. "What is all this?"

"Fynn and I decided that today is a great day to celebrate," he explains. "Your father is awake. And, you are the best thing that ever happened to us. What more could we want?"

"You guys..." I cup his face with my hands and give him a smooch on the lips.

"So, you just rest and relax in the tub, everything you need is here, but if we missed anything, there's a bell you can ring for assistance."

He points at an actual little bell next to the wine glass, and I chuckle out loud.

"You guys really thought of everything," I wink. "You're amazing."

"And, that's not all."

"Seriously?"

"Fynn's cooking dinner," he tells me importantly. "I'm just the helper. You know I'd burn the house down if I cooked on my own."

"Sounds about right," I grin. "Alright then. I shall go enjoy myself, and I'll see you in a bit for dinner."

He closes the door behind him, and in a few minutes, I find myself sinking into a full bath filled with hot, bubbly water. The feeling is divine. But, it's not only the bubble bath, and the scented candles, and the dinner. It's them. It's always been them.

I glance at the door, hoping to hear their voices from the kitchen, but the door is shut. I still smile, and sink deeper into the water, letting its velvety smoothness enshroud me. After a short while, I wash myself and quickly rinse off. When I walk upstairs to my bedroom, I see a little red dress laid out nicely on the bed. Next to it, there is a little note, with a rose attached to it.

Wear this.

Feeling as giddy as a fifteen year old madly in love, I hastily jump into this curve hugging dress, and put just a little dash of make up on. I walk over to the mirror, smiling. Not only smiling, beaming with happiness. The person looking back at me looks like a completely different person. She is confident. She is daring. She is fearless. She has found everything she has ever wanted in life, and more.

Raking my fingers through my hair loosely and adjusting my waves a little, I walk downstairs. There are pots and pans everywhere, on the kitchen stands, the counters, the island. Fynn is bending over the stove. The oven light is on. When he turns to me, I see he's wearing an apron, and I can't resist giggling.

"You guys really went all in, didn't you?" I walk around the kitchen island, and approach Fynn. "Mmm, you smell like chicken."

"What about me?" Anderson suddenly closes the fridge door, and he appears again in my field of vision.

He gets near me, and gives me a peck on the cheek.

"You smell like cake," I smile. "Oh, my god, you guys. You baked a cake?"

"Would be nice, no?" Anderson laughs. "But, no. We just ordered it."

"Still," I nod. "You guys are amazing. Putting all this together."

"It's still not done," Fynn tells me, walking over to me, and wrapping me up in a big, bear hug. "You go to the dining room, and sit your little self down. Dinner will be ready in fifteen."

"Are you sure there's nothing I can do to help?"

"No way, Jose," Anderson shakes his head, then proceeds to push me gently out of the kitchen and into the dining room.

Only then do I see that the dining room has also been decorated. There are candles everywhere, nestled in our old candle stands. I wonder where they found them. But, I'm lucky they did. The curtains on the big window are drawn, the lights are dimmed. There is soft music playing in the background.

"This is absolutely incredible," I say, as Anderson pulls a chair and sits me down at the table.

They proceed to set the table with a full blown four course meal, and by the end of it, I feel stuffed like a Christmas turkey. But, I know there is something else I want a taste of.

"Follow me," I tell them teasingly, as I head to the bedroom.

Once we're there, I point at them to sit on the bed, one next to the other. I play some soft music, and I start undressing for them, seductively stepping out of my dress and letting it drop to the floor. I turn away from them, unclasping my bra, as the straps glide down my arms, and off my perky little breasts. One arm is keeping them from plain sight, the other throws my bra at the guys. Anderson chuckles, and Fynn remains calm, his eyes focused on mine.

Then, my fingers find the thin line of my dainty, lace underwear, and I bend over slowly, bewitchingly, pulling down my panties as I do so. I've never done anything like this. I've only been with one man before Fynn and Anderson, and the last thing I could ever call myself was adventurous in bed. But, seeing the way they look at me, like I'm the most beautiful thing in the world, fills me with unsurpassed courage and confidence. I want to be everything for them. I want to make them happy and fulfilled in every single way a woman can fulfill a man. Or, two.

I stand up, leaving my panties on the ground. Taking a little sigh of encouragement, I turn around. Slowly, step by step, I walk over to them. I've never felt more confident, more desired than I'm feeling now. I help them out of their shirts, out of their pants, until we're all left completely naked.

I go onto the bed first, making sure to move slowly and deliberately. I prop myself onto my knees, my legs spread wide, giving them a good look of my wet pussy. Anderson jumps at the opportunity as his open mouth flies towards it, but I shake my finger at him.

"I want you to fuck my brains out," I tell them, biting my lower lip, allowing my cheeks to overtake the color of red completely.

There is no shame anymore, no embarrassment. I know what I want, and I want it now.

My own hand slides down against my lower belly, even lower, playing with my curls, my finger sliding between my soft, pink folds.

"I'm so wet for you..." I moan.

"Fuck..." I hear Anderson mutter, and his cock is erect, strong, begging to dive into me. "Got any more condoms?"

"No," I shake my head. "You don't need it."

"But..." he starts.

"Neither of you needs it," I tell them.

"I won't be able to pull out," Anderson admits, and Fynn nods as well.

"I know you will take care of me," I tell them. "That's why I want you to do everything to me. But, I need you to do it now... now..."

I moan some more, as my fingers spread my pussy even more, juices already leaking down my inner thighs. They change places, and I find Anderson in front of me, and Fynn grabbing at my hips.

"You're so fucking perfect," Fynn says as he spreads my ass cheeks.

I hiss loudly, my fingers digging into the pillow, trying to smother my moans. Fynn's fingers are playing with my pussy, my hardened clit begging, all swollen and needy. Anderson's cock is in front of me, and I lick the cream off the top of it. He moans, his voice like music to my ears. I don't want to take it slow this time. I want them to own me, every part of my body, as well as my heart.

"Put it in your mouth," Anderson instructs. "And, swallow every drop of my hot seed."

I see his thickness in front of me, and the fingers of my hand can't really fit around his entire girth. The thought of him filling me up with it again makes me shiver with delight. Fynn notices, and continues to play with my pussy, not wanting to fuck me still. The anticipation is too much. I'm walking between pain and pleasure, but I know the pleasure will be all the greater if I wait just a little longer.

I lick Anderson's cock again, my tongue tasting more of him this time. My fingers slide down his length, then back up. His cock is tense now, waiting, eager. His fingers find my hair, raking through it, grabbing a handful, but he doesn't dictate the tempo. I do.

I open my mouth and let him slide in. My lips close around him, tightening. He goes in a little deeper every time, my tongue flat against his base. I take more of him in, feeling him all the way in the back of my throat. I'm full of him. And, at that moment, Fynn enters me, spreading my ass and pussy as wide as he could. I feel like I have relinquished all control to them, and yet, it still gives me a strange sense of power.

I groan with pleasure, and Anderson feels the vibrations of my throat on his cock.

"Fuuuuck..." he moans, as his hips buck into me, digging deeper.

I start sucking him off faster, as Fynn keeps fucking my brains out – just the way I wanted them to. Fynn's hands grip my ass, slapping it occasionally, leaving dirty, red marks, which I can't wait to see in broad daylight. Hot flames surge through my body, my pussy begging for release, as I become a plaything of these two men who have taught me the true meaning of living.

I feel helpless in their hands, spread on the bed, completely naked, completely owned. Fynn thrusts into me hard, and I get lost in the sensation, bucking backwards against him, as he hits that sensitive spot no one has ever touched before. He adds a thumb to this winning combination, brushing it softly first against my clit, just to tease me.

Pleasure peaks inside of me. My entire body shakes, but I know I won't fall. I'll never fall as long as I have them to hold me. So, I fully let go, with Fynn fucking my drenched pussy and with Anderson's bulging cock in my mouth. My head is swimming with all the adrenaline. My pussy welcomes every ripple of ecstasy they send my way. It feels like my fingers are charged with electricity, and I finally come.

Panting, trembling, I'm a hot mess of my own juices. Fynn keeps fucking me mercilessly, and I hear him groan my name. His fingers dig into my flesh, but I don't feel it. I've lost track of time and space. There is only now, only this moment. Nothing else exists.

A moment later, Fynn thrusts into me hard, harder than before, hissing loudly. Anderson waits patiently, as I grab his cock again with my hand, jerking him off, while sucking. He cums in one big gush right into my mouth. I choke a little, but I manage to swallow it all in one gulp. Both of them are still buried inside of me. We're all still moving, going, but our motions are getting slower and slower.

Our bodies rock together in the force of that peak. So many sensations have passed through my body that I was barely able to keep track of them all. Breathing heavily, we drop down onto the bed, and the whole room is still spinning. I'm too shaken from that orgasm to be able to think straight, let alone speak a coherent sentence.

Luckily, we don't need to speak. Everything's been said already. We fall asleep hugging, dreaming of our future together.

Chapter 30

E pilogue – 5 years later
"I swear, I look so bloated, I feel like a whale," I huff and puff looking at myself in the mirror.

My hands are resting on my bulging belly, which protrudes from my flowery summer dress that I just put on. I'm due in a month, but it feels like I'm due in a week.

The twins are 3, and we all decided that it would be nice to keep all the siblings relatively close in age. So, here we are. Pregnant – again.

"You look gorgeous," Anderson reminds me, approaching me from behind, and wrapping his arms around me. "And, you smell like a snack."

He growls playfully, then pretends to bite me in the neck, knowing that makes me giggle like a school girl. He is still the one who can always make me smile, no matter how bad I feel. He'll always have that something.

"Don't," I lower my neck, and try to push him away, laughing. "You might wake up the twins."

"You know they sleep til late," he tells me. "And, besides, Fynn is in the kitchen. If they wake up, he'll hear them."

I know he's right. But, today is an important day, and I want everything to go smoothly. I don't want them to wake up cranky, and then make the whole day miserable for everyone else because they're tired. Toddlers can be so wonderful, and at the same time, so exasperating.

"Is everything ready for today?" I wonder, looking out the window.

The view of the mountain is spectacular. Only this time, I see our garden filled with a big wooden table, chairs and a few other things which hint at a little party.

"For lunch with your dad? Of course. Why wouldn't it be?" He shrugs his shoulders.

"Well, it's his first time coming down here," I explain. "I want it to be perfect. I want him to like where we live."

As it was to be expected, my dad first wanted us to live with him, in the mansion. It makes all the sense in the world, really. Especially for him. He wanted to have his family close. But, of course, the guys wouldn't even hear of it. It was the mountain house for them, and I have to admit, I liked that idea as well. What better place to raise children than at the foot of a beautiful mountain?

"Why wouldn't he like it?" he smiles. "I mean, this is Heaven on Earth. Especially now that you're here."

He makes me blush with his comment, as he usually does.

"I don't know... it's that I need for him to approve of it," I smile.

"I think no matter how old you get, you'll never stop being daddy's girl," he hugs me. "And, that's OK. As long as you allow us to love you equally."

"Of course," I hug him back.

We stay like that for a while, just hugging. Even the baby decides to take part, and kicks a few times.

"Whoa there, cowboy!" Anderson moves away and presses his hand against my belly. "That's some kick."

"Try feeling it from the inside," I chuckle.

At that moment, the door opens, and Fynn peeks in. His face is slightly sun-kissed from all the time we spend outside here. Surprisingly, he has been hands on with the twins, just as much as Anderson is. Even though, I can't say I expected that. He always seemed like he'd be the type of dad who would just pat his kids on the forehead, tell them they're doing a good job, then retire to his study. But, he has surprised me – in so many ways.

He walks over to us, and smiles.

"How are we doing today?" he asks.

"Still pregnant," I grin.

"Still glowing," he replies.

"Oh, you," I pinch his cheek. "I was thinking – "

But, I'm not allowed to continue. Someone is shouting from the room across the hallway.

"Looks like they're up," Anderson sighs. "I'll go get them. Meet you downstairs in the kitchen."

With those words, he leaves the bedroom, and gives us a few more moments alone. I appreciate every second spent with my men, especially because they are sometimes gone for a bit longer, and the house always feels so empty without them. However, that makes our time together all the more precious.

"You know what occurred to me this morning?" Fynn suddenly asks me.

He is standing in front of me, wearing a shirt and trousers. He has dressed up for today. I appreciate it, because I know how much he dislikes it.

"What?"

"I never thanked you."

I look at him, puzzled, not sure what he's referring to.

"Thanked me for what, Fynn?"

"For saving me."

His words are soft. I can tell they're coming straight from the heart, from some inner pocket that he's never opened before. Not until now.

"Where is this coming from now?" I smile at him gently, cupping his face with my hands.

His eyes are cavernous, gazing at me like I'm a well of beauty and power.

"You've given me so much," he continues. "You've changed me in more ways than one. And, I never thanked you for the most important thing."

"You can thank me now..."

He goes down to his knee, and takes my hands into his. He brings them to his lips, and covers them in a bunch of little kisses. Then, he presses my hands to his cold cheek.

"Thank you..."

His words seal the air between us, filling it up with love, gratitude, adoration. I help him up, and we hug each other tightly. My nose digs into his neck. My stomach pokes at his. But, nothing matters, as long as I have him, and Anderson, in my arms.

I want us to stay together like this, always. I want all of my breaths to be linked with theirs. I want always to be able to keep listening to their hearts beating the sound of my name.

Always.

Always.

Always.

Enjoy what you read? Please leave a review!

Don't miss out!

Visit the website below and you can sign up to receive emails whenever Lilly Wilder publishes a new book. There's no charge and no obligation.

https://books2read.com/r/B-A-KAQD-VEVWC

BOOKS 2 READ

Connecting independent readers to independent writers.

Did you love *Wolf's Mate*? Then you should read *Wild Wolves*[1] by Lilly Wilder!

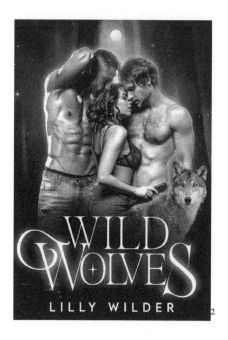

[2]

After the death of my mother, I have been thrust into the middle of a feud between two rival werewolf packs.

Hayden's return to town, after abruptly ending our relationship to play the field, started me down a path that I wasn't prepared for.

Faced with the truth about him and his brother, I found myself as the target of a rival pack's vengeance, causing me to seek safety with the man who broke my heart.

The bond that unites us is like nothing I've ever known, but will it be enough to heal the wounds of the past?

Trusting Hayden and Dante after our painful past seems impossible but it may be the only way for me to survive.

---

1. https://books2read.com/u/mv9rP8

2. https://books2read.com/u/mv9rP8

Will the three of us be able to stop fighting against our destiny or will we watch as everything crumbles down around us?

Also by Lilly Wilder

Indebted To The Vampires
Wolf's Nanny
Bearly Familiar
Protected by the Wolves
Bear Protection
Dragon Dreams
Seduced by Dragons
Her Lion Protectors
Rescued By The Wolves
Captured By The Dragons
Academy For Vampires
Her Biker Wolves
Bad Boy Dragons
Wild Wolves
Wolf's Mate

Milton Keynes UK
Ingram Content Group UK Ltd.
UKHW010639040324
438885UK00001B/136